ENGRAVED IN STONE

To Ella, Olivia and Flora,
You all are as toothsome
as spun sugar. May you
live happily forever more!
Alice S. Coleman

by Alice Scovell Coleman

illustrations by Anjalé Renée Armand

Tiara Books

Acknowledgments

First and foremost, I want to thank my sisters, Nell Scovell and Claire Scovell LaZebnik, writers extraordinaire. Although I am their older (not bigger) sister, I've learned so much from them. We may not be Charlotte, Emily and Anne, but I'm sure we laugh a lot more than the Brontës ever did.

I also want to thank the family members and friends who read the book and gave me advice and encouragement. So thanks to (take a deep breath before reading aloud): Mel and Cynthia Scovell, Gail Aidinoff Scovell, Julie Kaufman, Jennifer Damsky, Melissa Hayden, Charlotte Rasmussen, Elizabeth Weitzman, Amy Appleton, Diane Darst, Ellen Salant, Roxana Stix Brunell, Lisa Onofri, Caroline Berry, Sarah Kagan, Nancy Zachary, Jane Marino, Valerie Gelber, Cindy Frank, Lisa Rodman, Barbara Lavery, Rikki Kaplan, Eunyce Lipnick, Nerissa Radell, Julia Roshkow, Amy Berman, Linda Sousa, Margaret Smith, and Janie Fitzgerald.

I want to express my gratitude to the following knowledgable people who were so generous with their time: Alexander Isley, Julia Richardson, Monica Wellington, Carol Weston, Mark Gompertz, and Susan Raab.

Special thanks to Susan Berger who insisted on taking both of my girls on a Sunday so I could have a day to myself. This book might never have been started without those few quiet hours.

And a final thank you to Kevin Perrault who not only helped with the book's technical and design issues, but also kept Anjalé fed, watered, and happy.

Engraved in Stone
Text and illustrations copyright © 2003 by Alice S. Coleman
All rights reserved. Published by Tiara Books, LLC.

For information regarding permission, write to:

Tiara Books
62 Birchall Drive
Scarsdale, NY 10583

ISBN 0-9729846-0-7

Library of Congress Cataloging-in-Publicaton Data
Coleman, Alice Scovell
Engraved in Stone/by Alice Scovell Coleman

PRINTED IN THE UNITED STATES OF AMERICA

This book is dedicated to people from...

My past: my Granny and Buddy, the perfect complementary couple. Granny was so smart that Buddy couldn't believe she chose him, and Buddy was so handsome that Granny couldn't believe he chose her. Their love never faltered.

My present: my husband Stuart who makes me feel like a princess every day. (So where's my diamond tiara?)

And my future: my three children, Emma, Teddy and Libby, who allowed me to write even though it meant unmade beds, unwashed laundry, and uninspiring dinners. Their support and enthusiasm were essential and appreciated.

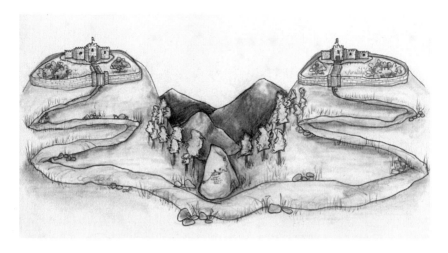

CHAPTER ONE

The STONE

There was a great tumult° in the two castles that stood on opposite hills overlooking the valley. In the white castle, the servants hurried about the kitchen, peeling and paring, stirring and stewing, baking and basting, mincing and marinating. The long banquet table was draped with lace and set with delicate porcelain and heavy silver.

In the gray castle, the servants scurried about the bedrooms, tucking and tidying, sweeping and swabbing, plumping and polishing, sponging and sprucing. The ballroom's marble floor gleamed brightly and the golden sconces° were filled with tall white candles.

In each town adjoining the castles, the hustle and bustle continued. All the villagers, from the loftiest aristocrat to the humblest beggar, donned their finest clothes and carefully wrapped their gifts, whether large or small, modest or extravagant. In every hand was a gray envelope containing a white invitation which read, in elaborate gold lettering, as follows:

° tumult: commotion, uproar
° sconces: decorative wall brackets

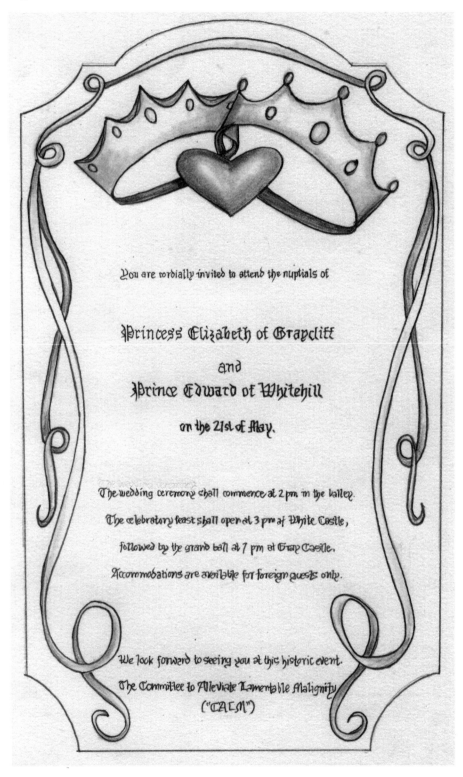

You are cordially invited to attend the nuptials of

Princess Elizabeth of Graycliff

and

Prince Edward of Whitehill

on the 21st of May.

The wedding ceremony shall commence at 2 pm in the valley.

The celebratory feast shall open at 3 pm at White Castle,

followed by the grand ball at 7 pm at Gray Castle.

Accommodations are available for foreign guests only.

We look forward to seeing you at this historic event.

The Committee to Alleviate Lamentable Malignity

("CALM")

Excitement and joy were in the air; smiles could be seen on all faces save two: those of Princess Elizabeth and Prince Edward.

❧ ❧ ❧ ❧

Scowling, Prince Edward tugged at his embroidered white tunic, and turned to his wrinkled chief advisor, Sir Robert.

"Explain to me again why I must go down to the valley today to marry a woman I do not love; nay, I do not even know."

Sir Robert sighed, "Your Highness, we have been over the importance of this marriage countless times."

"Yes, but never have we discussed it on the actual day when all is being readied and I am wearing a ridiculous outfit." He tugged again at his elegant clothes.

"Be still, Sire, and I will retread° well-worn ground for you. As you know, approximately sixteen years ago, when you were born, all was well in Whitehill. Your good parents, lively King Louis and lovely Queen Louise, ruled their people justly and wisely. Their best friends were the rulers of Graycliff, wise King Will and winsome° Queen Willa, parents of Princess Elizabeth who was born the same day as you. Inspired by the royal friendship, the people of both kingdoms lived in harmony and prosperity°.

"Then, one fine summer day when you were but a year old, a terrible tragedy occurred. Your parents and Elizabeth's arranged to meet for an outdoor feast in the valley. Each couple rode down their respective hills in elegant carriages and both, unfortunately, were exceedingly punctual. They arrived at the center at the same time and each set of horses, seeing the other oncoming set, went wild. The charging carriages collided with a large rock in the valley and all the passengers were killed instantly." Sir Robert paused and shook his head sadly. He continued, "The only rays of sunlight in the dark days that followed were the offspring each couple had left behind. The

---

° retread: review, go over
° winsome: charming, endearing
° prosperity: wealth, success

4

people of Whitehill and Graycliff deeply mourned the loss of their benevolent° rulers, but they rejoiced that time would furnish them with suitable replacements.

"Of course, people can be impatient and, without the example of the royal friendship, the inhabitants of Whitehill and Graycliff began to squabble. At first the differences were over minor matters like the proper shape of women's hats and the suitable length of men's tunics. Later, the disagreements became more significant and widespread. Disputes arose over fishing rights in the streams, hunting rights in the woods, and gathering rights in the groves. Arguments erupted over athletic competitions and cultural events. Each kingdom wanted to feel superior, and tensions grew so high that war seemed imminent°. It was then that I, as your guardian, and Lady Claire of Graycliff, as Princess Elizabeth's guardian, organized the 'Committee to Alleviate° Lamentable° Malignity.°' We knew that 'calm' had to be restored or all would be lost.

° benevolent: kind, generous
° imminent: about to happen, upcoming
° alleviate: make more bearable, lessen
° lamentable: regrettable, sad
° malignity: great ill will, extreme malice

"Our committee met often, studied the problem carefully, and concluded that a permanent link between the two kingdoms was necessary. That is why you and Princess Elizabeth were betrothed° to each other, to be wed before attaining the age of sixteen. And to ensure that the bond was immutable°, Lady Claire and I traveled far to Engravia to bring back a stonecutter. The Engraver carved the terms of the betrothal on the very stone where both unfortunate sets of monarchs lost their lives. Ever since the carving was finished, the people of both kingdoms have been pacified°."

Prince Edward responded angrily, "Perhaps the people are pacified, but I am not. Surely, our subjects have had ample opportunity to realize that they can live together in harmony without the completion of this marriage."

"You may be right, Sire, but unfortunately, once such terms are 'engraved in stone,' they cannot be altered. The carving creates a magical obligation which must be discharged."

"You leave me no alternative; I must escape from here. You've often advised me to be a man of action. Now I will prove my mettle°. I will leap from my window, swim the moat, climb the wall and flee to freedom."

"An excellent plan, Your Highness, were it not so stupid. The fall from the window probably would crush you, the alligators in the moat most likely would eat you, the stone wall undoubtedly would cut you, and the castle guards presumably would catch you. Not to mention the minor issue of the magical engraving. Perhaps you have forgotten that if you ignore its dictates, you and Princess Elizabeth will turn to stone. So talk no more of escape or delay. Your sixteenth birthday is on May 27th—less than a week away—and we can postpone the wedding no longer."

° betrothed: engaged to be married
° immutable: unchangeable, absolute
° pacified: soothed, calmed, placated
° mettle: spirit, bravery

Prince Edward looked crestfallen°. "I see I have no choice but to be led like a sheep to the slaughter°."

"I think you will find your fate a great deal more agreeable than that. Princess Elizabeth is very beautiful and highly accomplished."

"Prithee° tell me why have I not been allowed to meet her? Perhaps she is 'very beautiful' compared to a warty toad and 'highly accomplished' compared to a mossy stone."

"No, Edward, the only reason you have not met Elizabeth is that the Committee thought it best for you to learn to love each other once you discharged your duty to marry. But rest assured, she is the woman of your dreams."

"You mean she has long golden hair, laughing blue eyes, and loves sailing at dawn and horse-back riding at dusk?"

"Sire, I cannot guarantee any particulars, but I promise you that Elizabeth is an extraordinary person.

"And that extraordinary person will be my wife in just an hour's time," groaned Edward as he glanced at the clock. Still feeling like a condemned° sheep, he added a "baa, baa" and looked out his bedroom window to the gray castle in the distance.

❧❧❧

Staring out her bedroom window at the white castle in the distance, Princess Elizabeth wailed, "In just an hour's time I shall be wed." Her elderly chief advisor, Lady Claire, nodded in assent as she straightened Elizabeth's lace veil and smoothed her white silk dress.

Elizabeth turned to check her appearance in the room's full-length mirror. She smiled approvingly at her reflection which displayed her beautiful clothes and lovely face. Then she remembered the reason for her finery and turned away, frowning.

"How I dread this alliance°. There must be a way out."

° crestfallen: sad, dispirited
° slaughter: killing
° prithee: please, derived from "pray thee"
° condemned: sentenced to punishment
° alliance: union, cojoining

"Your Highness, you know there is not. The marriage is engraved in stone."

"Yes, yes, but there must be some means to escape. You have always advised me to be a woman of reason. Now is the time to test my powers. I will sneak down to the stone and alter its message, or perhaps, I will destroy it altogether."

"A very fine plan, my dear, were it not so foolish. I have never heard of a promise being altered once it is in stone, for the engraving creates a magical commitment that cannot be defied. Certainly, the only person who could even attempt such a feat would be the Engraver who has special tools and skills. But Engravia is far away, the route is treacherous, and time has run out. As for destroying the stone, you'd sooner be able to topple this castle. If the impact of the two carriages caused neither a chip nor a budge, how do you propose to demolish it?"

"Then I shall be forced to walk the pirate's plank and plunge to my watery death."

"I think you will find your fate significantly more pleasant than that. Prince Edward is very handsome and highly accomplished."

"I fear that he is 'very handsome' compared to a slithering snake and 'highly accomplished' compared to a rotted tree trunk."

"No, Elizabeth, you needn't worry. I dare say Prince Edward is the man of your dreams."

"Does he have wavy black hair and pensive° brown eyes? Does he love to read poetry at dawn and hear madrigals° at dusk?"

"Your Highness, I cannot guarantee any specifics, but I promise you he is an extraordinary person."

"And that extraordinary person will be my husband in just a blink of an eye." Still feeling like a doomed prisoner at sea, she added a "splash, glub, glub," and turned back to gaze out the window at the crowd gathering in the valley below.

° pensive: thoughtful, brooding
° madrigals: songs in two or three part harmony sung without instruments

CHAPTER TWO

The CEREMONY

To a great flourish° of trumpets and a swell of cheering from the crowd, Prince Edward stepped from his carriage into the center of the valley. From sheer habit, he smiled and waved at the assemblage°, although his heart was heavy. Edward's gaze was immediately drawn to the massive, engraved rock. Next to the rock, a platform had been erected for the ceremony. It was beautifully decorated with garlands of white flowers festooned° between poles. Except for the elaborate flower arrangements, the platform was empty. No sign of the bride. Then Edward remembered that Elizabeth's carriage was scheduled to arrive five minutes after his to avoid any accidents.

Sir Robert followed Edward out of the carriage, took his elbow, and escorted him through the crowd to the platform. Edward suddenly felt sick: his legs were shaky, his throat was dry, his hands were cold, and his brow was burning. Sir Robert sensed Edward's

° flourish: lavish display, fanfare
° assemblage: crowd, gathering
° festooned: draped

8

discomfort and led him to a large tent beyond the platform to re-cover. Edward closed his eyes and took some deep breaths. He felt better. Then he heard the blare of trumpets and shouts from the crowd. He moved to the flap of the tent and looked out in time to see the door of the Graycliff carriage open. His heart pounded as he thought, I will finally see my bride.

A slender figure in a white gown stepped out, but she wore a heavy veil that obscured° her features. She was accompanied by a gray-haired woman who guided her through the crowd toward the platform. Given their slow progress, Edward guessed that Elizabeth's knees were as wobbly as his own.

ह्ल ह्ल ह्ल

Elizabeth gazed through the lace veil as she walked slowly toward the platform. Everything had an odd white overlay—the faces she passed looked like they were caught in a heavy snowstorm. Even with her obstructed view, she was quite certain that the platform was empty. No glimpse of the groom, but the Whitehill carriage was present. Realizing that he must be close, Elizabeth suddenly felt ill: her legs were leaden, her throat had a lump, her palms were sweaty, and chills ran down her spine. She managed to croak out, "Water," and Lady Claire led her past the platform into the tent.

Elizabeth's eyes had to adjust from the glare of the sun to the dark of the tent. She sensed two figures standing, but could not see their features. As she raised the veil, her eyes focused and she found her-self staring directly into the face of a young man. He had straight blond hair and mocking blue eyes. She had to admit Prince Edward was quite handsome, but in a foolish tournament knight way.

Edward stared back, his eyes locked with the girl's. She had wavy black hair and serious brown eyes. He had to admit that Princess Elizabeth was quite lovely, but in a grave schoolmistress way.

° obscured: hid, concealed

Prince Edward broke the uncomfortable silence with a sly smile. "Why, Sir Robert, she is everything you promised and more." Elizabeth's heart leapt at the praise. Edward continued, "Yes, how could a man not attach himself for life to such a stunning creature?" Then Edward rushed across the tent and threw his arms around the elderly Lady Claire.

Lady Claire and Sir Robert laughed at Edward's joke, but Elizabeth smoldered° at the insult. Extricating° herself from the bear hug, Lady Claire said, "Allow me to introduce myself. I am Lady Claire and this is my ward, Princess Elizabeth of Graycliff."

Stiffly, Edward bowed and Elizabeth curtsied. Lady Claire continued, "I had promised the Princess a drink of water, so if you'll excuse me, I'll go fetch it."

"Let me assist you," insisted Sir Robert, and with a meaningful glance between them, the two left the tent.

Edward cleared his throat. "Would you allow me to ask a question of my future wife?"

"I don't think you should address it to me. Shouldn't you ask your wrinkled, gray-haired bride?" responded Elizabeth, her brown eyes flashing.

"It appears she couldn't resist the charms of Sir Robert and has deserted me. I am crushed, of course, but perhaps you will help me overcome my grief."

"Can't you take anything seriously?" asked Elizabeth.

"Can't you take anything humorously?" responded Edward. Elizabeth just glared.

Edward softened a bit. "No offense was intended by my joke, so no offense should be taken. Let's not waste this brief opportunity to get acquainted."

Elizabeth shrugged, so Edward continued, "I love sailing and horseback riding. How do you feel about them?"

° smoldered: burned slowly
° extricating: releasing from an entanglement

Elizabeth did not have to think for a moment. "Sailing makes me horribly seasick and horses make me sneeze. But I love poetry and polyphonic° music. How do you feel about them?"

Edward was equally quick to respond. "Poetry makes me irritable and fidgety. Serious music makes me unbearably sleepy." Edward thought he had better try a sure thing. "How about a summer afternoon watching jousting?"

"Tedious°," she replied. Elizabeth thought she'd find safe ground. "How about a winter evening reading a book?"

"Odious°," he responded.

The disappointed Elizabeth cried, "This is terrible. I see we have nothing in common. If only this marital obligation could be undone."

"Finally something we agree on," declared Edward.

Sir Robert and Lady Claire returned, bearing a goblet of water. "Ah, I hear you are in agreement. Splendid, just splendid," said Sir Robert, congratulating himself on leaving the two young people alone. "Well, let us delay no further. Your subjects are waiting, as are the feast and festivities."

After Elizabeth had a quick drink, the group walked out to the platform. The young people were placed next to each other, and Lady Claire and Sir Robert took their places at the helm to conduct the ceremony.

"We are gathered here today," began Lady Claire, "to fulfill a promise made many years ago to the people of Graycliff and Whitehill."

"Indeed, at this historic event you will witness the joining together of Princess Elizabeth and Prince Edward, for the duration° of their lives," said Sir Robert.

° polyphonic: music that combines two or more melodies
° tedious: boring, tiresome
° odious: hateful
° duration: full extent, entire period

"Let us review the terms of the stone." Lady Claire gestured to the front of the rock, where all eyes turned. Lady Claire read aloud the words that were carved there:

YOUR JOYS ARE MY DELIGHT, YOUR WOES ARE MY SORROW, YOUR PRESENT IS MY DAY, YOUR FUTURE, MY TOMORROW.

IT IS PROCLAIMED AND PROMISED THAT PRINCESS ELIZABETH
OF GRAYCLIFF AND PRINCE EDWARD OF WHITEHILL SHALL
BE MARRIED FOR LIFE BEFORE THE AGE OF SIXTEEN.
THIS CONTRACT SHALL BE SEALED WITH A KISS.
FAILURE TO COMPLY WITH THE TERMS
OF THIS ENGRAVING WILL
RESULT IN THE PARTIES BEING
TURNED TO STONE FOREVER.

There was a general murmur throughout the crowd. A Graycliff courtier commented to a Whitehill maiden, "He's ever so lucky to get Princess Elizabeth." She responded, "What do you mean 'he's lucky'? She's the lucky one to get Prince Edward." People around them began hotly debating the issue, with everyone convinced that his or her ruler was the superior prize.

Sir Robert cleared his throat loudly and looked sternly at the unruly° crowd. When they finally settled down, he said, "As dictated by the stone, Elizabeth and Edward, you are to learn to live not only *with* each other, but *for* each other. And now, all we need to complete your union is a kiss."

Edward's heart was pounding. How could he bind himself forever to this haughty, cold person? But what choice did he have? Would he prefer eternity as a statue of granite?

° unruly: rowdy, disorderly

Elizabeth's head was spinning. How could she tie herself forever to this flippant°, insufferable person? But what options were left? Would she prefer eternity as a figure in marble?

The rulers' thoughts were interrupted by the growing noise of the crowd which had begun to chant, "Kiss now, kiss now."

Sir Robert gently whispered to Edward, "It's time, Sire. Do your duty."

Lady Claire turned to Elizabeth, adding, "Yes, Princess, you must, too."

Edward closed his eyes. He tried to conjure up° the image of the blonde girl with joyful blue eyes, but all he could see were blazing brown eyes staring out of a warty toad. He opened his eyes and leaned forward.

Elizabeth felt him getting near. She closed her eyes and tried to imagine the dark-haired boy with thoughtful eyes, but all she could see were teasing blue eyes staring out of a slithering snake. She opened her eyes and leaned forward.

She could feel the warmth of his breath. He could feel hers, too. All it would take was a touch....

"NO!" they screamed in unison as they drew back.

The startled crowd was immediately silent.

° flippant: superficial, frivolous
° conjure up: call forth, summon

"What is the meaning of this? Do you wish to ruin yourselves and your people?" demanded Sir Robert.

Prince Edward looked pale and he swallowed hard before addressing the crowd. "People of Whitehill and Graycliff, I know this interruption comes as a surprise to you. I assure you, it comes as a surprise to Princess Elizabeth and me, too. But it would be wrong for us to go through with this sham° of a marriage. The stone destroyed our parents' lives and now it threatens to destroy ours, too."

Elizabeth then spoke: "This day has been called a 'historic event,' but a wedding should be a joyous event as well. Prince Edward and I each have been bound to marry a person we barely know. Yet in our brief acquaintance we are both convinced that we will never like, let alone love, each other. I cannot believe that any of you would wish us to forego° all hope of personal happiness in order to fulfill this aged promise."

Prince Edward interrupted, "Of course, we would fulfill the promise if it were essential to the well-being of our subjects. Our duty, first and foremost, is to serve our people. However, you have proven over many years that our two kingdoms can live together peacefully and prosperously. You do not need this marriage to continue such mutually beneficial° behavior."

Prince Edward was pleased to see that, in the crowd, many heads were nodding in agreement. One little boy yelled out, "Don't kiss!" and the people laughed and took up the chant.

Lady Claire stepped forward and held up her hand to quiet the voices. "I am sorry to disappoint you all, but remember, what is engraved in stone must be done."

Elizabeth said defiantly, "Then the engraving must be altered. I will set off immediately for Engravia to bring back the Engraver to help us."

° sham: fraud, mockery, counterfeit
° forego: give up, sacrifice
° mutually beneficial: equally advantageous, jointly favorable

Lady Claire shook her head. "I cannot allow you to undertake this perilous° task. The road is full of hidden dangers. You might never return."

Edward nodded. "I agree that Princess Elizabeth should not go. She should remain here because she would never succeed. I, however, will succeed. An adventure like this needs a person of strength, courage, and action."

Elizabeth objected angrily, "Perhaps the journey requires someone with brains, not just brawn°. You will not succeed, but I will. This mission requires a person of intelligence, insight, and commitment."

"May I remind you that on the rocky road you won't be able to read your lofty books in a comfortable chair by a cozy fire?" sneered Edward.

"And may I remind you that on the treacherous trail you won't be able to watch violent tournaments surrounded by fawning damsels° and raucous° companions?" taunted Elizabeth.

While the two young people squabbled, Lady Claire and Sir Robert whispered to one another. Finally, Sir Robert intervened. "Lady Claire and I have conferred on the matter and have concluded that, before either of you can commit to go, you must understand the requirements of this journey. First, you will have to travel on foot. Most of the path is too rocky and narrow to make horses practicable°." Edward sighed inwardly at having to leave his beautiful black stallion in the stable, but he tried hard not to show his disappointment.

Sir Robert continued, "Second, you will have to travel without servants. It is acceptable to endanger yourself on a mission that is of vital personal importance; it is unacceptable to endanger another person who is wholly unconnected to your goal." Elizabeth grumbled

° perilous: dangerous, unsafe
° brawn: strength, muscle
° fawning damsels: flattering maidens
° raucous: rough-sounding, loud
° practicable: feasible, possible

inwardly at having to dress and undress herself, but she strove to conceal her annoyance.

"Finally," said Sir Robert, "and I dare say this is the hardest requirement, you will have to travel together."

"What?!" said Edward and Elizabeth, each looking at his advisor with disbelief.

"Yes, together," responded Lady Claire. "Sir Robert and I disapprove of either of you undertaking this journey alone. If, however, you agree to travel together to Engravia, we will sanction° the endeavor. We believe that your success depends entirely on a cooperative effort. You both bring different skills to the adventure, and we hope you will use them. So, Elizabeth, do you promise to travel to Engravia with Edward?"

Elizabeth's face was white. "I promise to allow the Prince to escort me."

"Edward, do you promise to travel to Engravia with Elizabeth?" asked Sir Robert.

Edward's face was red. "I promise to allow the Princess to accompany me."

"Good," said Lady Claire, "then I suggest that you return to your castles to pack a few essentials and reunite here in an hour's time. The sooner you begin your mission, the sooner it will end. Remember, you must return here and resolve the issue by the last stroke of midnight on May 26th." She then turned to the crowd. "And now this unusual ceremony, which indeed long will be remembered as a 'historic event,' has come to an end. We invite you all to enjoy the food, wine, song, and dance at the castles."

The crowd roared its response as Edward and Elizabeth walked back to their respective carriages and drove up their hills to prepare for the journey.

° sanction: endorse, authorize

ChAPTER ThREE

The JOURNeY

One hour later, Prince Edward stepped out of his carriage into the valley. This time, however, there were no trumpets or cheers to herald his arrival. The valley was deserted and silent.

Edward shook his head at Elizabeth's absence. Wasn't it just like a female to be late, even when punctuality was crucial? He would be sure to chide° her when she arrived. In the meantime, he drew out of his hastily stuffed travel sack a small ball, and began tossing and catching it.

Within five minutes, Elizabeth arrived in her carriage, dismounted°, and dismissed her driver.

"I was starting to think you wouldn't come. I hear the path is very dangerous and requires great endurance°. Perhaps you want to give up on this journey?" Edward said, continuing his game of catch.

"You cannot frighten or dissuade° me. I said I would go on this mission and I shall," asserted Elizabeth.

"Then I assume your tardiness can be explained by a momentous event. Let me guess...you got tied up selecting the perfect frock for meeting foreign royalty and facing mortal danger."

"I promised Lady Claire that I would arrive after you to avoid a 'violent encounter,' but I see that the delay did not spare me from

° chide: scold, reproach
° dismounted: got down, descended
° endurance: strength, stamina
° dissuade: discourage, talk out of

one. I might add that I used the extra five minutes to procure a detailed map for our journey. I see that you've used your free moments most productively," she said sarcastically, gesturing to the rising and falling ball.

"I often toss a ball. It allows me to clear my head, and it's good training for my reflexes. Here, let's test...yours!" and with that, Edward quickly threw the ball at Elizabeth. Luckily, she had put down her bag and her hands were free to grab it.

"Good catch," said Edward with genuine admiration.

"How dare you throw that ball at me? It was heading straight at my face," Elizabeth snapped.

"Oh, no harm was intended and no harm was done. Why don't you calm down and throw it back?" said Edward.

Elizabeth hurled the ball back with all the force she could muster. "Now can we focus on something important, or should we spend a few more hours playing games?"

"I'm all in favor of getting started." Edward put the ball away in his sack and slung it over his shoulder. He headed toward the clear-cut path that ran through the valley.

"Not so fast. I think you had better take a look at the map," said Elizabeth.

"Everyone knows that this path leads to Engravia," Edward called over his shoulder.

"Every *fool* knows that, but if you'll consult the map," said Elizabeth, unrolling the well-worn chart, "you'll see that, even at the fastest pace, the main path will take at least four days to go and four days to return."

"Would you permit me?" Edward reached for the map. Upon close examination, Edward had to admit that the main path to Engravia was long and difficult. The key in the map's corner, showing travel times between cities, estimated the main route between the valley and Engravia at four to six days.

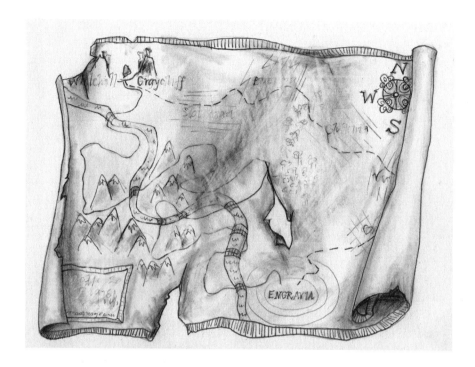

Edward shook his head in disbelief and said, "I guess we can't make it there and back before our deadline. I'd say our trip is over before it's begun."

"Now who's giving up on the journey?" said Elizabeth. "Look at the very small print in the box."

Edward squinted and read aloud, "Course of Challenges. Estimated travel time between the valley and Engravia: one day to a full lifetime."

Elizabeth prompted him, "Isn't that an improvement? We could make it to Engravia in just one day. We'll be back in plenty of time for our birthday."

"What do you suppose that 'lifetime' of travel means?"

"I really couldn't say, but since the Course of Challenges is our only hope of getting there and back in time, I suggest we take it."

She lifted her bag and strode over to a narrow, bramble-covered path leading up a hill. "And this is where we begin."

≈♠≈♠≈♠

The path was steep, overgrown and rocky, but the day was bright and the breeze gentle. After about an hour of hiking, Elizabeth broke the silence. "I think we should review what items we each brought. We should know what constitutes° our combined provisions°."

"You're right. We have to navigate incredibly rugged terrain°, but we should expend what little breath we have on chatting," Edward replied, annoyed.

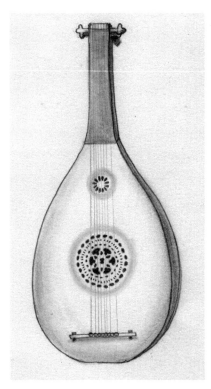

Elizabeth ignored him and began an inventory of her neatly packed bag. "Besides the clothes I'm wearing, I have a light cloak, an extra pair of stockings, the map, my dinner, a lute, a book of poetry, and my favorite dancing slippers."

"I thought we were instructed to pack only 'essentials.'"

"And so I have," replied Elizabeth.

"No doubt the world considers a lute and poetry, as well as dancing slippers, to be absolutely necessary equipment for a dangerous mission," said Edward.

Elizabeth spoke coolly: "My dancing slippers will be necessary if we are called upon to socialize."

° constitutes: makes up, forms
° provisions: supplies
° terrain: landscape, ground

"You really are anticipating horrible ordeals on this journey," moaned Edward.

"Would you please be serious?"

"I am being serious. I would rather face an enemy's army than be forced to dance. There's nothing more boring than barely moving in time to a dull beat. And I've suffered more serious injuries from la- dies' sharp heels than from knights' sharp lances. But pray continue your explanation; I can't wait to hear why your instrument and book were packed."

"I brought my lute and my book because hearing music and read- ing poems are like breathing air and drinking water to me. I depend on music to soothe and exhilarate° me. And I depend on poems, written by others and myself, to help me think about important mat- ters. The wisdom of the ages is often encapsulated° in a short stanza or two, and I read poetry to understand the world better. Now, per- haps you would deign° to share the contents of your bag?"

Edward looked at his messy sack. "Well, as you know, I brought my ball which is crucial for passing time when I'm kept waiting," he paused and shot Elizabeth an accusatory look, then continued, "and

a clean shirt, my dinner, a sword, which I'm certain will prove unnecessary, but will look dashing when I wear it, and most importantly, a bag of gold coins." He looked tri- umphant as he jingled a suede pouch that hung from the belt at his waist.

Elizabeth said scornfully, "I purposely didn't bring any

° exhilarate: excite, invigorate
° encapsulated: summarized
° deign: stoop, condescend

money. I'm sure that we'll be welcome to the hospitality of any realm we encounter, and I didn't want to expose us to any additional dangers on the road."

"I didn't decide to bring these coins frivolously°. While you were busy collecting your lute and poems, I discussed necessities with my Minister of Finance. He informed me that the Engraver is quite expensive and expects half payment in advance. So, you see, these coins are essential."

"If they are that important, I think I ought to carry them. You don't seem very adept° at holding on to things." Elizabeth gestured to Edward's messy sack out of which his shirt dangled precariously°. He colored slightly and quickly stuffed the shirt back in.

"I have no intention of relinquishing° this responsibility. I am perfectly capable of safeguarding these coins. I brought them and I will keep them," he said.

"Fine, just don't lose them. I rarely am wrong in my judgments, but I sincerely hope that I am in this case. The pleasure of being right won't outweigh the difficulty of being without funds." Elizabeth checked Edward's sack again for truant° items and, noting that it was quite full, inquired, "Are you sure that you've told me about everything you brought?"

"There is one other, unimportant thing," confessed Edward.

"What is it?"

"I'd rather not say."

"It is customary to comply with the request of any young lady, let alone a princess."

Edward knew this was true, but he refused to surrender. Maybe the journey would be over in a day or two and he could avoid the issue by stalling. "Why don't you ask me tomorrow?"

° frivolously: without serious thought
° adept: skillful, capable
° precariously: riskily, dangerously
° relinquishing: forsaking, handing over
° truant: runaway, fugitive

"Will your answer be 'yes'?"

"I give no promises," he said.

"Then you leave me no alternative: I command you to give full disclosure," she said sternly.

Edward stopped in his tracks. No one gave him commands. He was about to respond angrily, but he hadn't the strength for a long argument and decided to capitulate°, up to a point.

"Of course I shall obey, Princess Elizabeth. How could I resist your winning ways?" He reached into his sack. Elizabeth imagined he would produce a ribbon-bound packet of love letters from one of his simpering° admirers or some frightful weapon, but instead he withdrew a beautifully bound, thick book.

"As you can see, I have brought a book."

"I love books," said Elizabeth, reaching for the tome. "What is it about?"

Edward hastily drew the book back. "That's for me to know and you to wonder. This book is suitable for my royal eyes only."

Elizabeth cried, "I demand that you show it to me!" Her mind raced. What could the book contain that required such absolute secrecy from her? Were important state secrets concealed within its pages? Could Edward have plans to usurp° her throne and take over Graycliff? She held out her hand, palm up, and demanded, "Give it to me."

"Do you always get what you want?"

"Yes," said Elizabeth.

"When you want it?"

"Yes."

"With one exception," said Edward.

"With *no* exceptions."

° capitulate: give in, submit
° simpering: smiling in a foolish manner
° usurp: take over, seize

24

"Wrong. With *this* exception. This book is my property and it is private. You will never see it." Edward carefully placed the book at the bottom of the sack. "And now I suggest we stop talking and resume our journey."

Without another word, Edward began walking at a brisk pace. Elizabeth, who for a moment stood speechless with anger and disbelief, decided she would find a way to look at the book. She scurried to catch up.

❧❧❧

About two hours later, when they finally reached a level, grassy area, Edward declared he was starving and couldn't walk another step without nourishment. Elizabeth realized she was hungry, too, and agreed to pause briefly for a meal. The sun was starting to sink in the sky, and once darkness fell, they would have to stop for the night.

Elizabeth carefully laid down two cloths, one for sitting and the other for food.

"What dainty morsels did you bring?" asked Edward.

Lifting the cover from her meal box, Elizabeth said, "Pheasant in raisin sauce, popovers, custard, and a rare vintage of wine."

"A meal fit for royalty...or at least it was when we set out," Edward laughed.

Elizabeth looked down at her meal and saw that a few hours of heat, dust, and jostling had ill affected it. The pheasant had a greenish tinge and attracted flies, the popovers were deflated and soggy, the custard had separated into a watery mess, and the wine gave off a vinegary odor.

As she surveyed the inedible° items, tears sprang to Elizabeth's eyes. How could she have been so misguided in her selections?

Seeing her distress, Edward said, "Don't worry, I'll share my meal with you."

° inedible: cannot be eaten

"Really? Are you sure you wouldn't mind?"

"Actually, I'd prefer to give you some. Over the years I've discovered a secret: food tastes better when you share. Here, take this," said Edward, reaching into his bag and holding out a chunk of crusty bread and a slab of yellow cheese.

"Why, it's peasant food," said Elizabeth with disdain°. She waved her hand dismissively.

"Fine, don't eat it. More for me," replied Edward, withdrawing the offering and taking a hearty bite.

Elizabeth watched him chew and swallow, and bite off some more. Suddenly, her stomach felt even emptier. She hesitated a moment then, fearing that soon there would be nothing left, said, "On second thought, I would like a bit. Just to sustain my strength."

Edward shrugged and gave her a portion. From a ceramic jug, he poured some cool water into cups.

"This is the only food I'm willing to eat. I despise fancy sauces and exotic ingredients. Give me some simple, honest fare and I am content," said Edward as he finished his bread.

He passed Elizabeth a small, knobby apple and took one himself. After polishing it on his tunic, he took a bite. Elizabeth was about to comment that such apples were usually reserved for pig feed, but when she heard the apple crunch and saw its juices flow, she held her tongue. Although Elizabeth had never dined on such simple fare, she had to admit to herself that she had never enjoyed a meal more. It was wonderful to go from an empty stomach to a full one under the blue sky on a table of green grass.

Edward finished before Elizabeth and he tossed his ball while he waited. Elizabeth gnawed her apple right down to the core, then she flung it into the bushes as Edward had done. Elizabeth dusted the breadcrumbs from her lap, inadvertently° inviting a group of ants to join her. Immediately, Elizabeth raised her foot to crush them.

° disdain: scorn, contempt
° inadvertently: unintentionally, accidentally

"Don't do it!" cried Edward, rushing over. "What harm have they done you?"

"It's just a few horrid, intruding ants," she replied, with a slight shudder and her foot still poised.

"I beg your pardon, but *you* are the intruder. The ants live here; you're just visiting. Although I'm sure they're grateful for your offerings. Remember: food tastes better if you share."

"I have no intention of sharing with insects. I hate things that creep and crawl," she declared, but she did draw back her foot.

"I love studying them. I think observing nature helps me understand the world better. Just like your poetry helps you." He pointed to the busy ants which had formed a line and were retreating with pieces of bread. "Look at how well they work together and how hard each one labors. Why, those little creatures can carry burdens of eight to ten times their weight. It would be the same as me carrying a horse." He paused and added, "Although right now, I would prefer a horse to carry me." Edward rubbed his legs.

Elizabeth laughed. She had enjoyed watching the ants, but their industriousness seemed a rebuke° to her dawdling°. "With or without a horse, I think we'd better get going." Elizabeth stood up and was surprised to find that her legs were wobbly for the second time that day.

Seeing her rise, Edward picked up his sack and inquired, "Ready to go, then?"

"Only if my legs will move," she admitted.

"Just command them to do your bidding. That seems to work for you," he teased.

Instead of taking offense, Elizabeth, who felt too full and happy, laughed again. "If it would work, I would do it. But I suspect a quick rub and a stretch will be more effective." After a few

° rebuke: reprimand, scolding
° dawdling: wasting time, loitering

minutes of such ministrations[o], Elizabeth pronounced herself ready
to move on.

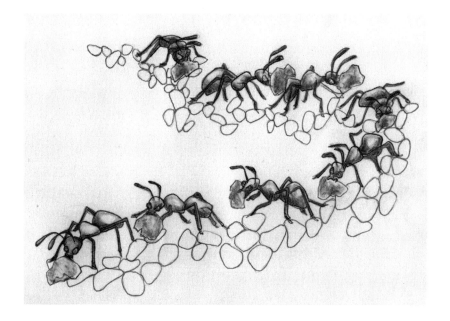

[o] ministrations: attentions

CHAPTER FOUR

SLOTHONIA

Up inclines they trudged, down descents they slid, over rocks they climbed, through brush they cut. Edward's sword proved quite useful, and not merely ornamental, in dealing with the abundant overgrowth.

Elizabeth's legs no longer wobbled, they ached. In fact, all of her ached, but she struggled to keep up with Edward and promised herself she would not complain. Edward was exhausted, too, but since Elizabeth kept a brisk pace, he promised himself he would not grumble. He did, however, keep a close watch on the setting sun, waiting eagerly for the moment they would have to halt their progress. He planned that, when it was time to rest, he and Elizabeth would use their bags as pillows and extra clothing as blankets.

As they rounded a bend in the path, his thoughts were interrupted by Elizabeth's shout of "A village!" And, indeed, just a short distance ahead stood a gated town with the inscription SLOTHONIA written in gray letters above the enclosure.

With renewed strength, the two ran to the gates and peered in. The village was unremarkable—it had the requisite° houses, shops and castle—save for three distinguishing features. First, everything was painted in shades of gray. Second, heavily padded benches were installed every few feet along the main street. And third, not a soul was visible.

"Do you think it's deserted?" Edward asked.

"There's but one way to find out. I'll knock," said Elizabeth, grasping a large knocker on the gate. She hammered the heavy piece and someone, who was sleeping on the bench nearest the gate, stirred. Elizabeth knocked again.

"Go hence," whined an old woman's voice.

"We will not go. We have traveled far today and need a place to rest. We command you to admit us," said Elizabeth.

"Not now," replied the voice, yawning.

"But we need help immediately. We demand your hospitality for the night," ordered Elizabeth.

"Get lost," the woman said, more pleading than angry.

Elizabeth decided to try a new tack. "Perhaps we should have introduced ourselves. I am Princess Elizabeth of Graycliff and my companion is Prince Edward of Whitehill. Surely your monarch would want to assist us."

"Move on," she beseeched° them.

Prince Edward shook his head and whispered to Elizabeth, "Sometimes, when words fail, actions succeed." He took hold of the knocker and began hammering without pause.

"Stop it," the old woman begged. She tried to cover her ears and rolled off the bench. As she hit the ground with a thud, her eyes opened. She slowly pulled herself up and shuffled over to open the gate.

° requisite: required, basic
° beseeched: begged, implored

"Come in," she said with resignation. Elizabeth and Edward entered quickly, fearing that the old woman lacked the strength to hold the gate open for long.

The old woman was quite a sight. Her eyes were heavy with sleep and her long gray hair was wild from the pillow. From head to toe, she was dressed in gray. She seemed kind enough, though, now that she was awake, just weary.

"Join me," she said and led them down the main street toward the castle.

"Where is everybody?" asked Elizabeth.

"In bed."

"Isn't it awfully early for everyone to have retired?"

"Need sleep."

"Yes, I'm sure they do. To be honest, I'm so tired I think I could fall asleep on this hard road and not wake up for a week. But luckily we found your village and will not have to spend the night outdoors." Elizabeth prattled° on about the difficulties of travel, hoping her words would keep the old woman awake. She noticed that the woman's pace had slowed and that every time they passed a bench, the woman looked at it longingly.

Finally, they arrived at the castle and entered. Inside, everything was shades of gray. Elizabeth rather liked the peaceful, bland interior.

The old woman led them across the vast, gray marble floor of the foyer to the wide main staircase. "Up there," she said, pointing at two doors on the upper floor.

"Are those our accommodations?" asked Elizabeth.

The old woman nodded. "For you," she answered, then she headed to the door. "Good night," she said and slipped out.

"Why do you suppose that old woman spoke so little?" asked Elizabeth as they ascended the stairs.

"Worn out," replied Edward.

° prattled: talked idly, babbled

ॐॐॐॐ

When they reached the second floor, they opened the doors and discovered identical gray bedrooms. Each room contained a spacious, curtained bed outfitted with luxurious gray linens. In front of a gray marble fireplace stood a carved armchair with thick pillows and a matching footstool. The cool night air was warmed, not by a cheerful fire, but by glowing gray embers in the hearth.

Calm music played softly and the air was scented with roses. A frilly flannel nightgown lay on one bed; a simple flannel nightshirt lay on the other. Both sleeping garments were gray.

"I guess this is my room." Edward gestured to the room with the nightshirt. "This certainly is preferable to sleeping on the road. I'll see you in the morning, bright and early."

Elizabeth nodded; she felt too tired to speak. Now she could understand the old woman's reluctance to chat. She closed the door, undressed, and pulled on the nightgown. Although she wanted to crawl into bed immediately, she forced herself to take out her book of poetry. She always read before bed, and tonight would be no exception.

Down into the comfortable chair she sank and by the flickering light of a candle, she read a verse. She congratulated herself on defying Edward's prediction: here she was, reading a book in front of a cozy fire in a comfortable chair. She would defy his prediction of her failure, too, and would succeed on this mission.

After a few minutes of reading, Elizabeth closed the book and dragged herself over to the bed. Up into the tall bed she climbed, slipping between the silky gray sheets and soft gray blankets. She placed her head on the fluffy gray pillow, thinking, Everything is just as I like it. I could stay here forever.

Mixed with the quiet strains of slow music, she heard Edward's snores from the other room. This was the perfect opportunity to sneak into Edward's room and peek at his secret book, but Elizabeth was too tired to move. She barely had the strength to think how much she loathed the sound of snoring. As soon as she shut her eyes, she was asleep.

è❀·è❀·è❀·

In the morning, Edward regained consciousness slowly. Coherent° thoughts barely surfaced through the thick fog of drowsiness. How long had he been asleep? It felt like it had been days and he reached for his chin, half expecting to discover a full beard. He was relieved to find only stubble. What time was it? The room was still darkened by heavy drapes. There were no signs of people stirring—no footsteps in the hall, no smells from the kitchen. He hoped he had not overslept.

Edward knew he had to get up, but could not rouse himself. He tried to talk himself out of bed, alternating between ordering and cajoling° himself, but to no avail. In desperation, he tried conjuring up the image of his most recent tournament battle. He was on his trusty stallion, charging down the path with his armor gleaming and his lance ready. From the opposite direction raced another knight. Just before they collided, Edward moved to the right. As he recalled the movement, Edward imitated it, hurling his body sideways. He nearly fell out of bed, but caught himself on the edge. Edward was pleased to discover that he was now fully awake.

He rose and drew back the drapes, flooding the room with sunlight. It was another beautiful day and, fortunately, the hour was not too late. Judging by the sun's position in the sky, it was mid-morning. Edward hastily dressed, grabbed his bag, and ran into the hall to look for Elizabeth.

He listened at her door, but heard nothing. Elizabeth must still be asleep. He decided to allow her to remain so and, in the meantime, would explore the castle and thank his host for the restful night.

° coherent: rational, lucid
° cajoling: coaxing, wheedling

As he descended the stairs, Edward noticed that all of the windows boasted heavy, drawn drapes, and only a few stray shafts of light illuminated the darkness. The faint light and ubiquitous[o] gray gave the castle an eerie feel. A chill ran down Edward's spine.

When his eyes grew accustomed to the dark, he was able to see that padded benches were arranged along the edge of the foyer. Closer inspection revealed that many of the benches held sleeping people. Edward tiptoed across the floor to a large, open room.

Over the entrance, a sign read "WAITING ROOM TO see The KING." The room, which was also entirely in gray, had numerous settees and chairs with over-stuffed pillows. On one settee slept a noblewoman propped up by her two napping children. In an armchair snored a hunter with his large gray dog dozing at his feet. Across from him slumbered a foreign emissary[o] wearing a gray turban, gray robes, and gray slippers that curled around-and-around at the toes. Off to the side, dreamt a maid, clutching her inactive gray feather duster.

At the far end of the room, by a massive gray door, slept two members of the royal guard. Finally, the throne room. Edward crossed the waiting room swiftly. Posted by the door, he saw a pale gray paper with dark gray lettering which read:

The ROYAL SCheDULe
MAY 22nd

7:30 AM	LOLL IN BED
8:30 AM	SLEEP AT YOUR POST
9:30 AM	IDLE CHATTER
10:30 AM	CAT NAP
11:30 AM	WHILE AWAY THE HOUR
12:30 PM	SIESTA!
1:30 PM	DILLY DALLY
2:30 PM	NOD OFF
3:30 PM	VISIT DREAMLAND

[o] ubiquitous: everywhere, ever-present
[o] emissary: ambassador, foreign representative

4:30 PM	FRITTER AWAY TIME
5:30 PM	TAKE YOUR EASE
6:30 PM	FEEL DOG TIRED
7:30 PM	TURN IN / FULL NIGHT'S REST AFTER A LONG DAY

Edward was amazed to see such a full, yet unproductive day. He glanced at a table clock; it read 10:23. Perhaps the king would grant him an audience since there were no apparent rivals for the honor.

Not wanting to disturb the guards, Edward pushed the door open himself. Inside he found another room of gray, this one with a cushioned throne that was reclining. The king was dozing as his Minister of State droned° on about the rising cost of lavender soap.

° droned: spoke in a dull tone

Edward couldn't blame the king for losing interest in such matters; he himself had often drifted off during Sir Robert's discourses. Edward cleared his throat loudly and the minister turned around. "Ah, young guest, have you come to converse with the king?"

"Yes, I have. I wanted to express my appreciation."

"Excellent. And who shall I say is calling?"

"Prince Edward of Whitehill. And to whom am I indebted?

"To King Listless of Slothonia." Hearing his name spoken, the king stirred. The minister seized the opportunity and shook him rather roughly. Then the minister pushed the throne into the upright position, severely jolting the king, and said, "Sire, you have a visitor. Prince Edward of Whitehill."

The king awakened, stretching and yawning, and the minister added, "May I remind you, Sire, that this is your hour for idle chatter. I hope you'll use it unwisely. And now, if you'll both excuse me..." The minister gave a yawn, and walking over to one of the chairs in the room, sat down, closed his eyes, and fell asleep.

"My gracious, people here seem to need a lot of rest," said Edward to the king who perfectly matched the décor. The king had a long gray beard, flowing gray hair, and tired gray eyes. Even his skin, in the pale light, seemed gray.

"Yes, we attend to the necessary repose° of all our people and visitors. Our motto is," said the king, pointing to a gray banner hung over the throne, "Let no one leave Slothonia...tired."

"As a weary traveler who has benefited from your philosophy, I want to thank you. Princess Elizabeth and I spent the night in unparalleled° comfort."

"Speak nothing of it. I'll be happy to accommodate you for as long as you'd like."

° repose: rest, relaxation
° unparalleled: unmatched, unequalled

"That you have already accomplished. Elizabeth and I have little time to travel to Engravia and back. I'm afraid we must take our leave this morning."

"Nonsense. You would miss all the fun—the cat nap, siesta time, dreamland." King Listless rubbed his hands together gleefully.

"It all sounds very appealing after yesterday's trials, but I'm afraid we must decline."

"Then let us turn, in our precious remaining moments, to unimportant matters. What do you know of the rising cost of lavender soap?" inquired Listless.

"I really couldn't say...."

"I hear that," the king said in a slow, dull voice, "with the decline of rainfall in the north, the output of lavender has decreased, causing a supply shortage. At the same time, the increase of rainfall in the south has caused inordinate° amounts of mud, boosting the demand for soap. As a result of the lowered supply and greater demand, the price of lavender soap has risen from three cents to four per bar, an increase of one-third over the pre-rainfall price."

Edward felt his eyelids drooping. He was about to slide to the floor to sleep when a vison flashed in his head: himself as a gray marble statue. How well he would blend in with the surroundings. Forever. His eyes flew open and he interrupted the monarch, saying, "Very fascinating, King Listless. Unfortunately, I really must be going."

"But we haven't begun to discuss the color scheme for my new royal robes. I was leaning toward dove gray with charcoal gray trim, but my minister was urging slate gray with steel gray trim. What do you think?"

Edward was about to respond, "I really couldn't say," but then he remembered the disastrous results he had garnered° from that reply. The king was already reaching for some gray fabric swatches, so

° inordinate: excessive, unrestrained
° garnered: gained, earned

Edward spoke quickly: "I think that a dove gray robe with dove gray trim would be best."

"Wouldn't that be awfully bland?" asked the king.

"I'm afraid that the contrasting trim scheme might be too loud. I'd stick with a monochromatic° outfit."

"Delightful idea. I must send for the royal tailor immedi..." The king stopped mid-word with a look of horror on his face. "What's wrong, your Majesty?"

"Look at the time. Oh, this is terrible," lamented the king. Edward looked at the gray table clock which read 10:32. The king continued, "I am woefully behind schedule. How will I ever catch up on the two minutes of sleep that I lost? No wonder I feel so exhausted." And without a "good journey" or even a "good bye," the king pushed his throne back and began to snore.

Edward was greatly relieved. It was high time he and Elizabeth set forth. He intended to move rapidly through the common rooms, but by the time he reached the foyer, he felt drowsy again. He was sorely tempted to lie down on an empty bench, just for a moment.

He headed toward one, but in the dim light, he did not see a gray tabby cat curled up on the floor. Edward stumbled over the cat, nearly falling on his face, and regained his balance just in time.

° monochromatic: having only one color

Once again, he was fully awake. He took advantage of his alertness and bounded up the stairs to the bedroom hall.

❧❧❧❧

There were still no sounds emanating° from the room. Edward rapped quietly, but getting no response, tried harder. Finally, he opened the door, calling, "Elizabeth, are you there?"

Her room, like the rest of the castle, was still dark. Edward walked to the drapes and opened them a crack. At first, he didn't see Elizabeth, she was so buried in the blankets and so still, but then he noticed her dark curls in the sea of gray.

"Elizabeth, it's time to rise," he said gently. She barely moved. "Elizabeth, we are late and must get started," he said more loudly and firmly. This time, she turned over. "Elizabeth, wake up!"

Her eyes opened, but they were unfocused and dull. "Can't I sleep a little more? I am still exhausted and need energy for the journey. What difference will a few minutes make?" Elizabeth pleaded.

° emanating: coming, originating

"I guess you're right. You need to be rested, and we're already late. Take a few more minutes." He had barely finished his words and her eyes were closed.

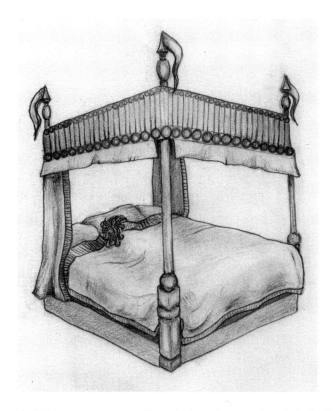

Edward did not want to disturb her by tossing his ball, so he reached into his sack and removed the thick book. He thought how Elizabeth would love to be looking over his shoulder. Worried that she might be spying, Edward glanced over at the bed. The dark curls hadn't moved. He opened the book.

After about ten minutes, Edward put the book away and took out his ball. He would play with it in the hall while Elizabeth dressed. Then Edward opened the drapes fully, but the bright light had no effect on the sleeping princess.

Edward tried speaking to her again, urging her to awaken. She slept. Exasperated, Edward propped up her slender body on the fluffy pillows, and she opened one eye.

"Go hence."

"Elizabeth, you must get up."

"Not now."

"But we're losing precious time."

"So what?"

"You want this mission to succeed as much as I do. Bestir° yourself."

"Need sleep," she said with a yawn.

Edward was worried. Elizabeth was as lethargic° as everyone in Slothonia. Her stupor° was even deeper after her short nap than before it. It seemed as though she could sleep forever. As slight as she was, Elizabeth could not be carried to Engravia and, given his promise to travel with her, she could not be left behind. Clearly, the only option was to force Elizabeth to fully awaken. He would have to get her moving. But how?

Edward smiled to himself as he took his ball from his pocket and tossed it in the air a few times, clapping his hands together noisily each time he caught it.

"Get lost," Elizabeth said, her voice drifting.

"Just testing my reflexes, and now it's time to test...yours." Edward threw the ball at Elizabeth. She caught it right before it hit her face.

"I cannot believe you threw that ball at me again," she screamed, her eyes alert and angry.

"Oh, no harm was intended, no harm was done. Why don't you throw it back?"

° bestir: rouse
° lethargic: sluggish, inactive
° stupor: daze, state of unconsciousness

"You bet I will!" said Elizabeth, springing from the bed and flinging the ball back at Edward. " I command you to take your ball and leave. I'd like to get dressed and resume our journey."

Edward replied, "Yes, Princess Elizabeth, how could I resist your winning ways?" but he did so with a smile. He was relieved to have Elizabeth back to herself, even if she was furious with him.

As they were leaving, Elizabeth suggested they go thank their host. Edward explained that the king had a very full schedule and could not be disturbed, but that, upon their return home, they should send him some lavender soap wrapped in dove gray paper and tied with a dove gray ribbon.

CHAPTER FIVE

ENERGIA

Outside Slothonia's gates, Edward and Elizabeth picked up the trail. Although they had slept soundly for many hours, they both felt sluggish and stiff. A cloud of drowsiness clung to them as they hiked, making progress slow and conversation impossible.

After a few hours of walking, they came upon a cool stream and drank eagerly. Edward saw with pleasure that their next meal was swimming in abundance in the clear water. Using his sword, Edward speared two fish. He cooked them over a fire of sticks while Elizabeth gathered ripe raspberries from nearby bushes. It was a modest meal, but Elizabeth made no objections.

Truth was, Elizabeth said nothing. Edward realized that she was still angry about the missile he had launched at her face. To make peace, Edward explained that he had found Slothonia perilous and that he had seen no alternative. Elizabeth acknowledged his need to rouse her, but she still fiercely objected to his violent methods.

Hoping to secure a more complete pardon, Edward told Elizabeth to wait while he hurried off to a meadow beyond a cluster of trees. He called back over his shoulder that he would return shortly.

Elizabeth immediately eyed Edward's sack. She knew it was wrong to look at something expressly forbidden to her, yet she had to know what the book contained. What if it held vital information? She might be safeguarding her own life or the happiness of her subjects. Surely, no one could fault her for seizing this opportunity to investigate. The trees would shield her from Edward's view and his sack was so messy that he'd never know she had rifled° through it. Edward would never be the wiser, but she would be.

Elizabeth quickly dug out the book; it was so heavy. Its contents must be very important for Edward to lug it on this journey. She hesitated for a moment. A ribbon marked one page. She would open to it at the ribbon, peek to make sure there was nothing dangerous, then put the book back immediately.

With trembling fingers, she parted the book's pages. She blinked several times, to make sure she was seeing correctly. There, staring at her, was a drawing of herself as she had appeared after last night's dinner, laughing, with her dark hair tumbled by the breeze. Edward was an artist and this was his sketchbook.

Elizabeth was flattered by this vision of herself; she particularly liked the intelligence and fire Edward had shown in her eyes. It was as though he had captured her soul on paper. She quickly turned the pages of the book. She found detailed sketches of rolling landscapes, charging horses, delicate flowers, even wrinkled Sir Robert. Everything was rendered with artistry and sensitivity.

"How dare you?" roared Edward.

Elizabeth jumped. She had been so absorbed in viewing the drawings that she had failed to notice Edward's return. He stood before her, his face red, clutching a bouquet of wild flowers in his hand.

Elizabeth felt more defensive than guilty. "You needn't be so angry. I don't see why you had to keep your drawings a secret."

"It doesn't matter why I didn't show them to you. I told you the book was for my eyes only. You had no right to look."

Elizabeth suddenly felt more guilty than defensive. "I dare say you're right. But you had me scared half to death that the book contained a plot for my overthrow. I'm sorry that I looked..." She paused. "But I'm also glad that I did. These pictures are so lovely."

° rifled: searched with thievish intent

Edward softened slightly with pride. "You really like them?"

"I really do." Elizabeth was relieved to see Edward's anger lessening. "Can you tell me about this one?" Elizabeth pointed to the open page. The drawing was of a small gray bird with a round belly, a pointed long bill, and long wing tips.

"I fancy you've never seen one of these little fellows," said Edward.

"I don't believe I have. What is it?"

"It's a white-rumped sandpiper, and it's quite uncommon."

"A rara avis," said Elizabeth.

"A what?" asked Edward.

"A rare bird, in Latin," explained Elizabeth.

"'Rara avis' sounds awfully fancy for something that looks so plain at first glance, but it is rather extraordinary. See how there are gray feathers on its back and breast? Underneath that dull exterior it hides a secret splendor: a pure white rump."

"When did you see it?" asked Elizabeth.

"Last summer. As I told you, I like to spend hours outside studying nature. But I guess that sounds foolish to you."

"It certainly is surprising. I always think of the outdoors as abounding in unpleasant things like newts and slugs and beetles. And then there is the matter of discomfort—it's often too cold or too hot, too windy or too still, too cloudy or too bright. But I would be willing to endure those tribulations° if I could make such drawings to share with others," replied Elizabeth.

Edward's face suddenly clouded over. "Just don't tell anyone about these drawings," he warned.

"Why not?"

"Because they're not for public viewing," he said.

There was Edward's reason for being secretive. "I know why you won't show your drawings. You don't want your wild tournament friends to know you're a talented artist."

"Maybe I don't."

"And you call yourself courageous," she scoffed.

"I'd be happy not to call myself anything if you would just stop talking," he snarled. Edward threw down the bouquet, grabbed the book and stuffed it in his sack.

"All right, I'll stop. How could I resist *your* winning ways, Prince Edward?" she said as she picked up her bag.

えるえるえる

Back on the road, Elizabeth looked eagerly for signs of a village. Her head was still heavy, and to clear it, she wanted a brief nap in a comfortable place. Eventually, although she did not see a village,

---

° tribulations: troubles, difficulties

she was greatly excited to hear sounds of people cheering in the distance. As the sound grew louder, Elizabeth and Edward spied another gated town. They hurried to the gates which bore the inscription ENERGIA in bright red letters that raced across the sign.

This time, before they had a chance to look in, the gates were flung open by a boy of about twelve with flaming red hair and bright red robes. Even his skin looked red from over-exertion.°

"Hello. So glad to see you. I am Prince Restless of Energia. Delighted you could come. Couldn't be more pleased. Really, I'm thrilled," he said very quickly and loudly. He grabbed Elizabeth's hand and pumped it vigorously up and down, then repeated the gesture with Edward.

° over-exertion: too much physical effort

Edward responded, "Nice to meet you. I am Prince Edward of Whitehill and this is Princess Elizabeth of Graycliff."

"Come on in. Don't hold back. We love to have guests. Perfect time to visit. Great events today. Huge excitement. Mustn't miss a thing. So much for you to see. So much for you to do." He barely paused to take a breath.

Elizabeth cut in. "Actually, I was feeling rather groggy and hoped you would have a place for me to take a short nap before we resume our travel."

"A nap? Nonsense! You need to get your blood flowing. You need to build your strength. You've come to the right place. You've come at the right time."

Elizabeth looked around and realized that napping here was out of the question. The village, which had a layout identical to Slothonia's, was a blaring tribute° to red. Everything was painted in the bold, brash color. The villagers, all attired in red, moved quickly from place to place and felt no compunction° about shouting to one another across the square. Eruptions of cheers and drum rolls were frequent. There was even an ear-splitting gunshot which gave Elizabeth quite a start, until Prince Restless explained that it merely signaled the beginning of a race.

In place of the padded benches lining Slothonia's main street, there were stations to test one's strength. These included log splitting, nail driving and pig lifting. Villagers of various ages and sizes participated.

"Your timing couldn't have been better. Today we have a competition. For athletes ages twelve to fifteen. You are eligible, right?" Prince Restless inquired. Edward acknowledged that, until May 27th, they both were fifteen.

° tribute: statement of admiration
° compunction: reluctance, uneasiness

"Capital! You must participate. Teams need four players. Two males, two females. My team, 'The Scarlets,' needs a male. 'The Vermilions' need a female."

Edward began to protest that they really didn't have time to play, but Prince Restless wouldn't hear of such objections. "The competition is every two years. Finally I'm old enough. If you don't play, I'll have to wait so long. Besides, you need activity. This will clear your heads. You'll be ready for the road. Please stay. It will be so much fun," Restless pleaded.

Elizabeth was about to decline, but Edward caught her eye and looked so desirous of a little recreation that she gave in, saying, "I guess we can stay a short while."

"Hurray!" screamed Prince Restless, and he jumped up and down, twirled himself around, and did a cartwheel. Elizabeth and Edward smiled at his youthful exuberance°.

"We must go to the playing field. Our competition begins soon. We can't forfeit for tardiness...." Elizabeth barely heard the last word for the young prince immediately broke into a run and was tearing through the crowd, down the main street, and past the castle. Elizabeth and Edward ran after him, not wanting to lose their way.

When they reached the noisy playing field, over which flew a red flag with the motto *"LET NO ONE LEAVE ENERGIA ...BORED,"* Elizabeth and Edward were handed loose tunics and shorts in the bright reds of their respective teams. They took turns changing into their outfits in a nearby tent, then met their teammates. The members of the other teams, the Crimsons, Roses, Cherries and Clarets, eyed the new entrants suspiciously.

The girls were competing first in long distance running. All twelve competitors were positioned at the starting line and told to run two laps around the large field. The winner would gain three points for her team; second place, two points; third place, one point.

° exuberance: enthusiasm, high spirits

Elizabeth had not been allowed to run since she was a young child. Lady Claire forbade any unladylike behavior, which included racing through the castle corridors, sliding down banisters, bounding up stairs, and climbing trees. A genteel stroll in the garden was deemed appropriate exercise for a princess. To behave correctly had been deeply inculcated° in Elizabeth, but she still liked to walk quickly and dance vigorously.

Elizabeth was nervous about the race. Her long, strong legs were untested, and she feared she would embarrass herself in front of all the spectators in the bleachers, and more importantly, in front of Edward.

The gun blasted, and off the runners flew. A girl from the Scarlet team, who was bigger and bulkier than Elizabeth, took the lead with smooth, steady strides. Elizabeth tried to pace herself, and found she could keep comfortably in second place. As they neared the finish, the Scarlet girl stumbled and Elizabeth tore past her. Elizabeth was surprised by how much she was enjoying herself—the sun felt warm on her back, the wind sang in her ears, the smell of spring filled her nose, and she could taste victory. Deafening cheers from the crowd greeted her as she crossed the finish line. Elizabeth discovered that the grogginess that had plagued her was gone; she felt clear-headed and alive.

Edward acknowledged her win, saying, "Not bad for a beginner. Now watch how a master does it."

Although Elizabeth was annoyed by his comment, she had to admit that he was a skillful runner. He looked like a deer, with his limbs moving easily and gracefully. Edward came in first, and the crowd went wild. Prince Restless, who was thrilled that his team was tied for first place, jumped up and down, turned himself around, and did a series of back flips.

° inculcated: instilled, ingrained

Next was pole climbing, in which Prince Restless and the Scarlet girl placed first and Elizabeth and Edward placed second. Both the Scarlet and Vermilion teams were unsuccessful at the javelin throw.

Then came wrestling. Elizabeth was shocked by the brutality of the sport; this was definitely an activity Lady Claire would condemn. Elizabeth asked to be excused from the round, explaining that it was customary for a young lady, let alone a princess, to eschew° such undignified conduct. Prince Restless would hear nothing of an exemption; her team would be disqualified if she withdrew.

Edward saw Elizabeth's face turn pale when she was called to the circle. He hastened to her side and whispered, "Think of something that really angered you. Use that anger against your opponent."

Elizabeth was paired against the burly Scarlet girl, who definitely had found her motivation. The girl believed her win in the running race had been snatched unfairly, and her anger was genuine, not imagined. As they grasped each other's arms, Elizabeth searched for her source of strength and focus. Then she thought of how Edward had humiliated her when they first met in the tent. How he had lifted her hopes with a seeming compliment, only to dash them with a childish joke. Her indignation° rose and her arms and legs felt powerful. In Elizabeth's mind, her opponent wasn't the Scarlet girl, but the mocking Edward of yesterday's meeting. With a mighty surge, Elizabeth pushed the other girl out of the ring. The crowd leapt to its feet and boomed its admiration.

Edward raced over to Elizabeth, saying, "Gracious, what did you have to be so angry about?"

Elizabeth smiled. "Nothing important," she answered and discovered that it really wasn't important anymore and never would be again. Now Edward's joke seemed funny, as did her triumph over her more worthy opponent.

° eschew: shun, avoid
° indignation: resentment, righteous anger

Edward fared equally well in his match. He thought of how Eliza-beth had accused him in front of all their subjects of merely having brawn, not brains. Without much effort, he defeated his Vermilion opponent. After the match, Edward realized that the insult, which had inspired his win, no longer stung him.

Elizabeth, who had joined in the cheering for Edward, suddenly felt drained. And it was getting late. She went over to Edward and Prince Restless and said, "We've had a wonderful afternoon, but we really must be going."

Prince Restless replied, "Folderol. Only one more event for today. You cannot leave now. Your teammates would be disap-pointed. The crowd would be devastated° . "

Elizabeth turned to Edward for support. "Tell him, Edward, how imperative° it is that we resume our journey."

Edward spoke almost as quickly and loudly as the young prince: "Actually, the sun has almost set. It seems a shame to go. We'll only have to stop. It's already late. What difference will one event make? We need to be energized for our journey. I've never felt so alert. I've never felt so strong. Let's stay to complete the contests."

Outnumbered, Elizabeth felt compelled to assent° to the princes' pleas. Unfortunately, the final contest was the high jump which would take a while to assemble. In the meantime, Prince Restless suggested, they could visit the arena next to the field to watch his knights in tournament battle. Edward eagerly agreed, but Elizabeth declined. She watched as the two princes ran off in the direction of the tournament.

At the arena, Edward found himself seated in a special box with Prince Restless, a few of his older, jovial° friends, and several bonny maidens. The young women all gushed about Edward's sporting

° devastated: distressed, highly upset
° imperative: crucial, urgent
° assent: agree, consent
° jovial: jolly, cheerful

prowess° and vied for his attention. The young men all yelled and screamed and moaned and groaned in response to the tournament triumphs and defeats. Edward was swept along with their enthusiasm and joined in vigorously. In a rare moment of quiet between matches, Edward congratulated himself on defying Elizabeth's prediction: here he was at a lively tournament, surrounded by appreciative girls and spirited comrades. He would defy her prediction of his failure, too, and would succeed on this mission.

ৼ৶ৼ৶

Elizabeth wandered around the grounds, looking for a quiet place to sit and rest. As she made her way through the boisterous° crowd which had descended from the bleachers, she was struck by the high level of noise and energy. It was after 8 PM, yet even tiny toddlers, who long ago should have been tucked in bed, were frolicking°.

° prowess: skill, ability
° boisterous: rowdy, lively
° frolicking: playing, cavorting

There were groups of people doing jumping jacks, while others did sit-ups or ran in place. Everyone was talking rapidly and loudly.

Elizabeth could not find a quiet, secluded spot. She was about to abandon her plan to rest, when she thought of the tent where she and Edward had changed their clothes. She quickly headed there.

Outside the tent, Elizabeth spotted a sign that displayed, on pale red paper with dark red lettering, the following:

THE ROYAL CONTEST
MAY 22

4:30 PM	LONG DISTANCE RUNNING
5:30 PM	POLE CLIMBING
6:30 PM	JAVELIN THROW
7:30 PM	WRESTLING
8:30 PM	HIGH JUMP
9:30-11:59 PM	GENERAL TRAINING

MAY 23

12:01 AM	LONG JUMP
1 AM	SHORT DISTANCE RUNNING
2 AM	DISCUS THROW
3 AM	WEIGHT LIFTING
4 AM	BOXING
5 AM	SUNRISE SWIMMING
6 AM	DIVING
7 AM	SOCCER

TO BE CONTINUED WITH NON-STOP EVENTS
UNTIL THE NEXT ROYAL CONTEST

Elizabeth looked at the schedule with horror. While technically Prince Restless had told them the truth that only one event remained that day, he had neglected to mention that there was more physical exertion planned for that evening and many more events as soon as tomorrow began. And when was the next Royal Contest?

Hadn't Prince Restless said it was in two more years? If they remained in Energia even a few more hours, Edward would be too exhausted to travel for days. And if they lost days of travel, their hopes of reaching Engravia would vanish.

More than ever, Elizabeth needed a quiet place to think and rest. She entered the tent and was relieved to find it deserted. She searched for their bags and found them next to a wheelbarrow filled with javelins. Using the bags as a pillow, she tried to close her eyes to rest. It was pointless. She was too alert to sleep and could scarcely sit still, even though she was exhausted from the day's exertions. She decided to settle for some contemplative° time, and took out her poetry book to write a bit.

After a brief interval, she heard Prince Restless calling her name, entreating her to rejoin her team for the high jump. When it was Elizabeth's turn at the event, clearing the bar was impossible—her legs were too weary to propel her fast enough and her arms were too weary to push her hard enough. She landed in the soft cushion and felt relieved that she had fulfilled her obligation, albeit without distinction.

Edward, however, was still charged up, and he easily cleared the bar as it was raised higher and higher. In his winning vault, as he sailed over the barrier, Edward thought, What a wonderful place this is. I could stay here forever.

The crowd's animated response further lifted his soaring spirits.

When the high jump was over, Elizabeth approached Edward and suggested they go rest. Prince Restless joined them, saying to Edward, "You don't want to rest. And you don't have to. We'll keep our muscles warm by exercising. We'll build up our strength. Then we'll continue the contest. There's weight-lifting. There's boxing. There's swimming. There's soccer. What do you think?"

"It sounds fantastic! I can't waste all this momentum."°

° contemplative: meditative, thoughtful
° momentum: forward movement, impetus

Just then, one of the bonny maidens jogged by and called out, "Prince Restless, how about I climb the pole and you see if you're fast enough to catch me?" The red-headed monarch was off like a shot.

Edward began jogging in place. The sun had set, and Elizabeth could barely see his face, but she could hear his feet as they rapidly pounded the ground.

Elizabeth spoke: "Edward, you really must rest. It's late, and we have a full day of travel before us."

"Elizabeth, I am getting so physically fit. What great training. I'll get to Engravia in half a day. Forget a full day of travel."

"That is ridiculous. We've already been traveling for over a day and we haven't reached our destination. Who knows how long it will take us to get there. But one thing I do know, if we don't resume our travel, we'll never make it."

"Elizabeth, you worry too much."

"Edward, you worry too little. You must stop this foolish activity."

" I'll only stop this foolish discussion. I'll save my breath for important things," and with that declaration, Edward launched into a series of rigorous squat-thrusts.

Elizabeth was distraught°. Edward was as frantic as everyone else in Energia. His excessive exertions were only increasing as the day wore on. It seemed as though he could exert himself forever. Given their differences in size, she could not physically force him to depart, and given her promise to travel with him, she could not leave him behind. But what could she do?

Then, inspiration struck. Elizabeth ran to the tent and dumped out the javelins from the wheelbarrow. They hit the ground with a thunderous clatter, and Elizabeth froze. She was sure the villagers would come running to stop her. But loud noises were the norm in Energia, and no one came. Once the danger had passed, Elizabeth changed into her clothes, loaded their bags into the empty wheelbarrow, and pushed her way on to the field. Torches with red flames

° distraught: distressed, worried, upset

bordered the field, giving the scene a warm, red glow. Elizabeth easily found her way back to Edward, who was now doing deep
knee-bends.

Elizabeth placed the wheelbarrow next to Edward and removed
her lute, poetry book, and cloak. She made sure that the two bags
formed a soft cushion inside the barrow.

She opened her book to the page where she had written while in the
tent, then she positioned her lute and strummed a few tremulous°, slow
chords. In a sweet, soft voice, she sang the words she had written:

> "Go to sleep, my weary one,
> Now close your heavy eyes,
> The time has come to rest your head—
> The sun has left the skies."

Edward stopped his deep knee-bends and stood still; she continued:

> "You've leapt so high, you've run so far,
> You've climbed and thrown and fought,
> The time has come to rest your head—
> You must do what you ought."

Edward sat down on the barrow, listening. On she sang.

> "All day you've toiled very hard,
> Indeed you've labored long,
> The time has come to rest your head—
> So harken to my song."

Lying down on the soft bags, Edward closed his eyes. Elizabeth
strummed. She had run out of her prepared words, but unfortunately, Edward was not yet asleep. He stirred. She had to sing one
more verse, and so she improvised.

> "Once more I'll urge you: go to sleep,
> Though I know it's a bore,
> The time has come to rest your head,
> I want to hear you snore."

° tremulous: quivering, shaky, timid

And right on cue, Edward obeyed. The sound, which the night before Elizabeth had found so loathsome, suddenly seemed one of the most beautiful she had ever heard. She rejoiced that, in their first interview, Edward had disclosed the effect serious music had on him. When his snores were steady and slow, Elizabeth covered Edward with her cloak; then she placed the book and lute inside the wheelbarrow and lifted its handles.

Pushing the heavy load through the crowded street was hard work for the tired Elizabeth, but she persevered°. She was relieved that the villagers were too busy with their own endeavors to notice hers. Finally, with her back aching and her hands rubbed rough, she passed through the gates and on to the road. She continued till she could no longer hear the shouts and cheers of Energia. The silence, disturbed only by Edward's snores, was delightful.

Elizabeth lay down on the hard ground with a rock for her pillow. She knew that, even with such an uncomfortable arrangement, she would sleep well. As she fell asleep, she smiled at a final thought. The people of Energia should add a new competition to the Royal Contest, one which required more endurance than running, climbing, throwing, and jumping combined: wheelbarrow pushing.

° persevered: persisted, kept trying

CHAPTER SIX

GLUTTONIA

As the sun peeked over the horizon, Edward and Elizabeth awoke. Edward was shocked to find himself flung atop a wheelbarrow with his limbs dangling over its sides.

"Why am I sleeping in this awkward, uncomfortable contraption?" he asked crossly, struggling to raise his stiff, achy body.

"Because it was necessary to remove you from the temptations of Energia, and I couldn't carry you." Elizabeth sat up and rubbed her sore arms.

"You mean to tell me that you pushed me through the town streets in this barrow?" Suddenly, more than his body, Edward's pride was hurt.

"I do."

"How could you make such a spectacle of me? I was a hero there. I was the greatest athlete those girls had ever seen." Edward turned his back, removed the scarlet tunic he was still wearing and donned his own.

"Perhaps you were, but if I had let you stay there a few more days, they would have had a marble statue of you to erect in the town square. Have you forgotten that we have only three and a half days to get the Engraver and return home? I think you should be thanking me for my efforts, not censuring° me."

"Maybe I did need your help, just like you needed mine in Slothonia, but you didn't have to make a fool of me."

"Well, you didn't have to imperil° me," retorted Elizabeth, her voice rising.

° censuring: criticizing, expressing disapproval
° imperil: put at risk, expose to danger

Edward tried to restore calm, "Clearly, we can't change the past, but let's promise that if another occasion calls for a rescue, we won't endanger or embarrass each other."

"Fine, that means you'll never throw another ball at my face."

"Right. And you'll never drag me around like a peasant with a load of potatoes."

At the mention of the word "pota-toes" Edward and Elizabeth froze; they were both starving from so little food and so much exertion°.

Elizabeth spoke wistfully: "What I wouldn't do for just one potato."

"Baked, with butter melting into its tender center," sighed Edward.

"I can almost smell the butter," said Elizabeth, sniffing the air.

"And fresh baked bread," added Edward.

"Huh, me too," said Elizabeth, surprised. She was afraid she was hal-lucinating°. "But that's impossible," she asserted, trying to rein in her imagination.

"Is it?" Edward quickly picked up his bag and ran to the top of the nearest mound. "Over there, just a short distance, is a town. I think the smells are coming from it. Let's hurry."

"I'm not sure that I have the strength to get there," lamented Elizabeth.

"Think of fresh, hot, crusty bread dripping with sweet strawberry jam."

"I'll race you!" she exclaimed, jumping up and grabbing her bag.

They quickly arrived at the village gate which bore the inscrip-tion GLUTTONIA in fat, white letters. Near the gate stood a table, covered with a white cloth, which held a white porcelain dinner bell and a white plate of white mints.

° exertion: effort, hard work
° hallucinating: imagining, having delusions

Elizabeth raised the bell and shook it gently. Immediately, a vision of white appeared. At first Elizabeth gasped at the ghostly figure whose skin was pure white. Then she realized it was a man covered from head to toe in a thin dusting of flour. His hair and mustache were white, as was his entire outfit which included a large apron and chef's hat.

"Oh, ze weary travelers 'ave arrived. Tres bon. I 'ope that you are both 'ungry," said the chef with a heavy French accent.

"Yes, indeed, we are very 'ungry, I mean, hungry," Elizabeth assured him.

"Zen, you must follow me wiz no delay. Ze queen 'eard of your approach from ze royal 'unters, and she is waiting to dine. But make no mistake, she does not like to wait."

The chef ushered them through the gate and they were dazzled by a world of white. Gluttonia was configured exactly like the other two villages, but along the main street were white tables covered with white cloths, topped with white napkins and white china. Seated at the tables, on white metal chairs, were stout, white clad villagers who were devouring the food in front of them. Everything smelled delicious, and Elizabeth and Edward needed all their willpower to follow the chef down the road to the castle.

"Why is everything white?" inquired Elizabeth as they walked.

"It is ze best color to set off ze beauty of ze food, and it does not distract. In Gluttonia, we like to focus on our food. Although I would like to focus on you awhile," the chef said to Elizabeth.

Edward interrupted, "I'm so hungry, I could focus on a whole cow."

The chef was excited. "Zen, I will be able to offer you 42 pounds of sirloin steak, 45 pounds of 'amburger, 45 pounds of swiss steak, 94 pounds of pot roast, 46 pounds of rib steak, 20 pounds of brisket, 20 pounds of marrow bones for soup, and 34 pounds of stew meat."

"Sounds like just a little bit too much," joked Edward.

The chef looked deflated. "Per'aps you are right." Then he brightened. "I know: I will omit ze soup!"

Inside the white castle, they crossed the white marble foyer to the banquet hall.

"I must leave you now. I 'ave many dishes to prepare." The chef turned to Edward. " I 'ope zat you find your visit 'ere most enjoyable." Then, he turned to Elizabeth and said, "You are as toothsome° as spun sugar. I wish I could stay wiz you but, alas, my culinary° creations must be my emissaries. I rejoice that my offerings will touch your tender lips." He kissed Elizabeth's hand, leaving a white mark of flour where his moustache touched, and sped away.

"If he cooks half as well as he woos, we're in for a fine meal," teased Edward.

"You're just jealous that I have ardent° admirers, too," responded Elizabeth.

"Not true. I'm all in favor of your having ardent admirers who will feed me. Come. Ze feast awaits us," he said, taking Elizabeth's arm and crossing the threshold into the hall.

The royal guards raised their white horns and blew a fanfare, announcing the latecomers' arrival. It was like the blast of an Energia gun starting a race, thought Elizabeth, as the guests grabbed their utensils and began eating. From the vigor with which they consumed the food, one would have thought the diners were starving, but their girth° belied° that conclusion. Everyone was dressed in flowing white garments that barely covered their large, rotund° bodies. Chins were numerous on each round face.

At the center of the long banquet table sat a most formidable° woman tucking into a plate of eggs and herring. She greeted Edward and Elizabeth, unfortunately, with her mouth full of food: "Welcome, welcome." Chew, chew. "I am Queen Bottomless of Gluttonia."

° toothsome: tasty, appetizing
° culinary: cooking
° ardent: passionate, eager
° girth: circumference, measurement around the body
° belied: contradicted, disproved
° rotund: round, plump
° formidable: fearsome, arousing awe

Swallow, sip of cider, new bite. "Not 'Bottomless' as in lacking a back-side..." Laugh, chew. "But 'Bottomless' as in pit." Laugh, swallow.

"Good morning, Your Majesty. I am Prince Edward of Whitehill and this is Princess Elizabeth of Graycliff. We are traveling to Engravia and seek a morsel to eat." He looked longingly at the table sagging with meats, cheeses, eggs, cakes, breads, and fruits.

"I'm afraid we can't help you with a morsel," replied the queen, pausing for a bite. Edward feared that she was unwilling to share even a crumb. "Because all we have are hearty portions," she said and laughed loudly, her numerous chins quivering and her open mouth displaying an unappetizing mixture of eggs and herring. "I don't know how you can stand there so patiently. We waited a full three minutes and twenty-four seconds for your arrival, and I almost cried from the hunger pangs. Here, come sit by me." She motioned with her laden fork to two empty places, flinging eggs in the air as she did so. Between the open-mouth chewing and the flying food, Elizabeth was starting to lose her appetite, but she reminded herself that she needed to stay strong for the journey.

Edward gallantly pulled out Elizabeth's chair, and then placed himself next to the queen. Politely raising her napkin, Elizabeth placed it in her lap.

"You're an amateur, I see," bellowed the queen. "Put your napkin where it will do some good." Elizabeth looked around the room and realized that all the guests had their napkins tucked under their multiple chins. They all seemed intent on consuming as much food as possible in as little time as possible. Elizabeth feared that the table would soon be cleared, so she reached quickly for a raisin roll.

Her fears were put to rest when, on her white plate, she discovered a heavy piece of white paper which read, in rounded letters:

THE ROYAL MENU, May 23

6 - 9 AM	BREAKFAST	
	eggs Florentine, candied bacon, jellied herring	
9 - 10 AM	MID-MORNING MEAL	
	a varity of cakes and ale, fresh and dried fruits	
10 - 12 NOON	LATE MORNING MEAL	
	cod stew, sausage, roasted apples, bread	
12 - 2 PM	DINNER	
	duck, leg of mutton, baked potatoes, apple tarts	
2 - 3 PM	MIDDAY MEAL	
	fruits, cheeses and breads	

3 - 5 PM	MID-AFTERNOON SWEETS
	cakes, custards, puddings
5 -6 PM	LATE AFTERNOON MEAL
	baked fish with mashed potatoes
6 - 9 PM	SUPPER
	potted beef, partridge in plum sauce, rice,
	carrots, pear tarts
9 - 10 PM	AFTER SUPPER OFFERINGS
	wine, cheese and wafers
10 - 12 AM	MIDNIGHT MEAL
	leftovers from all May 23 meals

"LET NO ONE LEAVE GLUTTONIA...HUNGRY"

Prince Edward studied his menu and said, "I don't normally eat such fancy foods. Could I possibly order some scrambled eggs and dark bread?"

The queen actually stopped chewing. "I set the finest table in the Western Hemisphere, probably in the world. I insist that you sample my dishes."

Edward reluctantly reached for an almond tart. He sniffed it. It didn't smell unpleasant. His stomach growled, demanding to be filled, so he took his first, tentative nibble. It was delicious. Edward put small portions of some of the dishes on his plate and tasted each one. Everything was delicious. He heaped large portions of all the dishes on his plate and dove in with gusto.

When he was ready to breathe again he turned to the queen. "This is the best food I've ever tasted in my life. I think I could finish everything on the table."

"Splendid!" exclaimed the queen. "A growing boy like you needs nourishment." Chew, chew. "You need a full belly to be strong and active." Swallow, sip, new bite.

"You are so right, Queen Bottomless. Yesterday I was competing in several events at Energia and..."

Queen Bottomless cut in, "Please stop talking, my dear, just con-centrate on your breakfast. Fewer distractions for you, fewer distractions for me."

As he resumed eating, Edward realized that no one else was speaking, although the room was far from silent. Instead of conver-sation, there was the clanking of silverware, the clinking of glass, accompanied by slurping, gulping, crunching, and gnawing. Fre-quently, there were outbursts when a guest would exclaim with a full mouth, "Yummy," "Delectable," "Delicious," "Scrumptious," "Fabu-lous," "Tasty," "Refreshing," "Luscious," or simply, "Mmmm." Such eruptions were tolerated as long as the inspiring dish was immedi-ately passed around for sampling.

At first, Elizabeth joined in the tastings enthusiastically, but after about two hours of trying delicious dishes, she began to feel full. Edward, however, showed no signs of slowing. He was completely absorbed in his plate, and whenever someone said, "You must try this," he complied. There were a few minor disruptions at the table—an elderly man belched loudly and a young woman briefly lost her bodice when the seams burst—but Edward was oblivious to them.

After three hours, in the middle of the late morning meal, Eliza-beth tried to speak to Edward quietly. "Edward, I think it's time we gave our thanks and bid the queen farewell."

"Elizabeth, did you try the honey cake? It's ambrosial°."

"No doubt. But you must be sated° by now, and we really must be going."

"I am not full." Chew, chew. "I've never been so hungry in my life. I just can't seem to get enough." Swallow, new bite. "I never knew food could taste so good."

"I'm sure they would pack us a meal for the road."

° ambrosial: exquisitely tasty; ambrosia was the food of the Greek gods
° sated: full, satisfied

"You know fine food can't travel. No, let's just stay here a while longer. We wouldn't want to miss the leg of mutton. Now let's stop talking. Fewer distractions for you, fewer distractions for me."

Elizabeth, however, was longing for distractions. A servant offered her some little heart-shaped cakes sent by the chef, but Elizabeth was too full to be tempted. She tried playing with the leftover eggs on her plate, pushing them into a mound and pretending her fork was a traveler climbing and descending the hill. She soon had to desist° because the nasty looks from her fellow guests told her that food was for consumption, not amusement.

Luckily, she did not have to wait long for a new diversion°. The court jester, clad all in white, including his silly, three-branched hat, walked to the center of the banquet hall.

"Hello, everyone. Nice to see all your chewing faces again. I see I got here 'jest' in time for brunch." No one stopped eating. "Let's see, why did the chicken cross the road?"

"To get to the other side," Elizabeth ventured.

° desist: cease, stop
° diversion: entertaining distraction

"No, so he could be baked in a white wine and tarragon sauce," answered the jester. There were a few grunts of approval from the guests.

"What's worse than finding a worm in your apple?"

"I know," said Elizabeth. "Finding half a worm in your apple."

"Wrong again. Finding *no* apple." Nods of agreement from the guests. "Why did the deaf man eat no fish?"

"Why?" responded Elizabeth.

"Because he was hard of herring." A few titters. "I ran into a vagabond on the road. He said he hadn't had a bite in weeks."

"So you bit him," interrupted Elizabeth.

"No, so I brought him home and gave him a seven course meal with wine." A general murmur of approbation°.

"Why did the escaped criminal eat only mutton?"

There was a pause. Elizabeth, realizing she was the only one willing to respond, asked, "Why?"

"Because he was on the lamb."

The queen actually laughed. Unfortunately, her mouth, as usual, was full of food, and she began to choke. Nobody at the table seemed to notice, except Elizabeth, who jumped up and handed the queen a glass of water. The jester knew he had gone too far and immediately stopped telling jokes. As soon as the queen was recovered and eating, he reached for two apples and an orange from the fruit bowl and began to juggle. The queen commanded him to stop using edible fruit which might get bruised and called for some slightly rotten items.

From a large container of rejected fruits, vegetables, and eggs, the jester selected an apple, an orange, and a pear. Then he began a dazzling display of juggling. He threw the fruit overhand, he threw it underhand, he sent it flying behind his back, he tossed it between his legs. He spun himself around, and still kept the circle aloft. Elizabeth tried to get Edward to watch, reminding him how much he enjoyed tossing a ball, but he refused to look up from his plate.

° approbation: approval, admiration

For his grand finale, the jester took bites out of the apple and pear while they spun in the air. Elizabeth was so impressed by the feat that she jumped to her feet, applauding enthusiastically. The disruption caused the guests to glare at Elizabeth, and the jester lost his concentration. He missed a catch and the orange went flying under the table near Elizabeth. Both she and the jester dove under the tablecloth to retrieve the errant° piece. Elizabeth got to it first. They remained under the table, happy to be hidden from all the disapproving eyes and moving jaws.

"Sorry for ruining your act," she said, handing the jester the orange.

"Please, don't be sorry. That's the first applause I've gotten in years."

"Tough crowd."

"Tougher than dried beef. I don't know why they bother to have me appear. They don't like distractions. But, since it pays the bills, I keep trying."

"It must be terribly frustrating."

"By my troth°, it is. One day, I was so sick of getting no response that I threw a cream pie in the queen's face. It splattered all over her. I was afraid that I was going to be the next thing to splatter, but all she did was laugh and lick it off. Seems a pie in the face is a pretty efficient way to get a pie in your mouth." He shook his head sadly.

"Does everyone always eat so much here?"

"Once they sit down at the table, they never seem to stop."

"And when do they get up from the table?" asked Elizabeth.

"Can't say that I've ever seen it happen."

"Oh dear, how am I going to get my companion away? We need to get to Engravia immediately."

° errant: runaway, roving
° troth: good faith, honor, word

"I really don't know. Perhaps if you distract him enough from his food, you'll be able to lure him from the table and then out the door."

Just then, very loud, rapid music began to play. The jester raised his voice. "It's the queen's musicians, 'The Beaters.' She likes them to play fast and loud. Says it inspires everyone to eat faster. Well, I'm done for the day." He handed the orange back to Elizabeth, saying, "I wouldn't want our conversation to be fruitless°," and then he was gone.

When Elizabeth emerged from under the table, she discovered that all new dishes had been set out. Edward had helped himself to heaping portions and, in response to the frantic tempo of the music, was shoveling food into his mouth. Elizabeth tried once again to persuade Edward to leave, but he rudely rebuffed° her. Elizabeth feared that, once again, Edward was caught in a spell. She must intervene, but how could she free him? She paused for a moment, thinking, then ran to her bag.

From its depths, Elizabeth withdrew her dancing slippers and cloak. She put on the slippers and swung the cloak around her shoulders. Then she stepped cautiously into the center of the floor.

In time to the lively music, Elizabeth began to dance. At first she felt self-conscious, and her steps were sedate° and courtly. Edward showed no signs of interest. Then Elizabeth became bolder. She twirled and whirled; she leapt and stepped. Edward looked up from his plate. Finally, the wild, fast music carried Elizabeth away, and she danced as if airborne with her cloak high over her head, billowing like a sail. Her heart was pounding and her brow was damp. Edward stopped chewing and put his fork down. Leaping over to his chair, Elizabeth moved her arm in a graceful arc and offered her hand to Edward.

° fruitless: wasted, unproductive
° rebuffed: rejected, refused
° sedate: cheerless, grave

Edward was spellbound. Elizabeth seemed like a fairy who could make him see the music with his eyes. He could not resist her extended hand, and she pulled him to his feet.

Elizabeth led him to the open floor and they danced together, spinning and swirling around the room. Edward had never experienced the freedom of dancing this way. He was intoxicated° by the blurry whirl of movement. As the music swelled, Edward lifted Elizabeth by the waist, and as he lowered her, they looked into each other's eyes. Elizabeth saw eyes that laughed without mocking, and Edward saw eyes that flashed without anger. They smiled. Edward placed Elizabeth gently on her feet and the music stopped. The guests began to applaud, and Elizabeth and Edward bowed to each other and then to the crowd.

Suddenly, the queen called out, "Corpus bones, the food is getting cold," and she picked up a piece of the rotted fruit from the container and threw it at the dancers. The guests followed suit. Elizabeth and Edward found themselves ducking and dodging many unsavory° missiles, but unfortunately getting hit by quite a few. They grabbed their bags and ran out of the banquet hall, as a moldy peach narrowly missed Edward's head.

They continued running until they reached the gates. Edward, who was trying to keep rotten egg yolk from dripping out of his hair into his eyes, said, "Well, I guess you broke your promise not to endanger or embarrass me in a rescue attempt."

"Not so," replied Elizabeth, surveying the rotten tomato covering her skirt. "We agreed not to endanger *or* embarrass each other, but I managed to endanger *and* embarrass you."

"A distinction worthy of Sir Robert. I guess, then, that I should be thoroughly grateful. I hope you'll permit me to show my appreciation Gluttonia-style," and with that, Edward scooped up a handful of mints

---

° intoxicated: overcome, excited
° unsavory: unpleasant, disagreeable

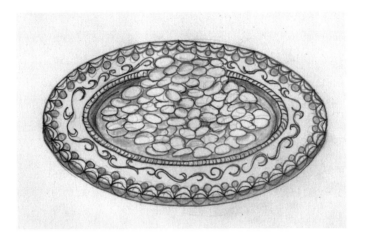72

from the table by the gate and began pelting Elizabeth with them. Elizabeth laughed, grabbed some ammunition, and retaliated°.

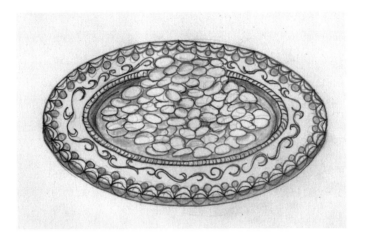

<hr/>

° retaliated: struck back

CHAPER SEVEN

VANITONIA

As the midday sun shone down on Elizabeth and Edward, their besmirched° garments began to emit a dreadful odor. Dirt clung to their sticky clothes and skin, and flies buzzed noisily around them.

"We had better clean up promptly or I shall have to banish myself from my own company," said Elizabeth, wrinkling her nose.

"You don't think we should stay this way? We could return home in this condition and start new fashion trends." Edward assumed the high-pitched voice of an older, sophisticated woman: "For spring, young men will glue down their hair with egg yolk. The look is guaranteed to attract the ladies and the flies." Elizabeth did not look amused, but Edward continued, "And for summer, young ladies will wear gowns adorned with colorful stains of rotted fruits and vegetables. The putrid° smell is guaranteed to ward off serious diseases and zealous° suitors."

Elizabeth shook her head and sighed, "The only consolation I have right now is that my friends can't see me."

"I can't imagine why you'd want to hide the Princess Elizabeth who wears dirty clothes, eats peasant food, and pushes wheelbarrows."

° besmirched: sullied, ruined, despoiled
° putrid: rotten, decaying, rancid
° zealous: eager, enthusiastic

"She would cower° in the closet right next to the Prince Edward who enjoys dancing, eats fancy fare, and draws beautifully."

"Let's not get into any closets together—we'd both faint from the stench°," urged Edward.

"You're right. We'll avoid all enclosed spaces until we've found a stream and washed our hands and faces."

"And hair," added Edward as he swatted away a fly hovering about his head. Edward's gaze followed the fly's path and was caught by unusual lights glinting in the woods. He pointed out the mysterious glowing spots to Elizabeth, and they soon discovered their source when another gated village came into view.

Above the gates, in elaborate silver lettering that reflected the sunlight, read the name *VANITONIA.*

° cower: cringe, tremble
° stench: disgusting odor

Elizabeth ran to the gate to ring the ornate silver bell, asserting, "I'm sure we can wash up here."

The gate was opened by a pretty, pert° servant girl clad in a silver dress and apron with a silver cap atop her head.

"Oooh, aren't we the messy ones? Been makin' mudpies, duckies? Well, it's into the bath with the both of you for a right proper scrubbin'. No arguments, mind you. Can't have you callin' on the princess lookin' such a fright. Send her to her bed from the shock, it would," asserted the girl in her cockney accent.

Edward replied, with a sly wink at Elizabeth, "We had no intention of bathing. But we will submit to your demand if it is required for an audience with the delicate Princess..."

"Flawless, ruler of Vanitonia," supplied the maid.

Edward said, "You may tell Princess Flawless that Prince Edward, the messy, and Princess Elizabeth, the untidy, eagerly await an introduction once they have removed the dirt of the road."

"Well, come on in, lambs, and let's get started. This dirt removal is lookin' like a major undertakin' worthy of many skilled attendants." The maid held the gate wide open, making sure to put as much distance as possible between herself and the odoriferous° travelers.

The inside of Vanitonia gleamed silver. Along the main street stood large mirrors with intricately° carved silver-leaf frames. Numerous villagers, all dressed in silver garments, gathered in front of the mirrors, jostling° for the best position to gaze at their reflections as they fixed their hair and adjusted their garments. Elizabeth was horrified when she caught a glimpse of her own reflection, and was greatly relieved that everyone else was too absorbed in self-scrutiny to make her an object of ridicule°.

° pert: lively, energetic
° odoriferous: strong smelling, pungent
° intricately: with complexity, with interwoven elements
° jostling: pushing, elbowing
° ridicule: mockery, derision

The interior of the castle was elegant and ornate. Everything was silver, lit by massive sterling candelabra° standing on mirrored tables. Huge mirrors adorned the walls, and Elizabeth had to avert her eyes repeatedly to avoid her own, unappealing image.

The chatty maid led Elizabeth and Edward up the staircase and there they parted, Edward to the care of male attendants, Elizabeth to the care of female.

Edward was ushered into a large bathroom with a silver tub in the middle. A warm, lemon-scented bubble bath had already been prepared. After eagerly removing his sticky garments, Edward slipped into the water. He closed his eyes and sighed contentedly. His relaxation was short-lived, however, for the team of male attendants swooped in and pounced on him. They came armed with brushes, soap, washcloths, soap, sponges, and more soap. Dirt was their enemy and they had sworn to vanquish° it. After lengthy scrubbing and numerous rinses, they pronounced Edward fit to emerge. He was wrapped in a thick, silver bathrobe, which soothed his reddened, raw skin, and led to a silver dressing room. There, the attentions continued: Edward's hair was trimmed and combed, his face was shaved, his teeth were brushed and polished, his ears were plumbed for wax, and his nails were cleaned, clipped and filed.

Edward obediently submitted to all the tortures, wanting to be really clean after being really dirty, but he drew the line when the head attendant came at his face with a large powder puff. The disappointed servant had to content himself with merely splashing lime scent on Edward's cheeks. The royal tailor selected a tunic of silver damask° with matching silver tights and shoes. Edward could not avoid seeing his reflection in the numerous mirrors on the wall, and he allowed himself a faint smile of approval at his greatly improved appearance.

° candelabra: decorative candlesticks with several branches
° vanquish: conquer, defeat
° damask: a richly patterned fabric, often silk

Edward was escorted to the hall to await Elizabeth's arrival, and he had ample opportunity to continue appreciating his visage°, for the hall was decorated from floor to ceiling with mirrors.

❧❧❧

Meanwhile, Elizabeth was being given the same, albeit more gently administered, treatment. After Elizabeth's violet-scented bath, the royal hairdresser styled her hair high on her head in a complicated cascade° of curls. The royal artist powdered her face, rouged her cheeks, reddened her lips and outlined her eyes. The royal seamstress fussed and fretted over the selection of a dress from among many silver frocks, each one more beautiful than the last. Elizabeth was forced to model all of them and even she, who admired splendid garments, began to lose patience, especially when she thought of Edward waiting for her. Finally, she declared the gown she had on her absolute favorite, although it was no better nor worse than any other, and refused to take it off. Matching shoes and fan were selected, and just when Elizabeth thought there was no room for improvement, the royal jeweler arrived. He adorned Elizabeth with a necklace, bracelet, earrings, and rings of diamonds set in silver. Then, for the final touch, he affixed a fiery tiara to her hair, and all the female attendants burst into applause. Elizabeth could not contain an ear-to-ear grin as she gazed at her reflection and basked in the unanimous° admiration.

When Elizabeth emerged, Edward was impatiently pacing the hall, with his back toward her. As he turned, she caught sight of his freshly scrubbed, glowing face and exquisite clothes. She laughed with delight. "My goodness!" she exclaimed, "you certainly do clean up well."

"Oh, I bet you say that to all the princes," said Edward with a blush that betrayed his pleasure at the compliment. "And you..." His

---

° visage: face, features
° cascade: waterfall
° unanimous: undisputed, undivided

voice trailed off. He was about to say, "look breathtaking," for indeed, he had gasped when he saw her, but he stopped himself and said, "Are a sight for sore eyes...but, unfortunately, that's not the only part of me that's sore." He gently touched his neck which was still red from rigorous scrubbing. He then asked, "What took you so long?"

"I was being held hostage by a team of skilled attendants dedicated to my physical improvement." She paused and added shyly, "Was it worth the wait?"

Edward, who was not accustomed to such discussions, answered, "I don't know much about dresses, but that one certainly looks nice."

Elizabeth, sensing that this was his version of high praise, took a turn blushing, and said, "Oh, this old thing—I found it in the back of my closet and threw it on. It does suit me, though, doesn't it? Although I don't think I'll be running any races in it. I can barely walk with all these petticoats!"

The veracity° of her statement was immediately proved, for the royal footman arrived and bade the two visitors follow him to the reception room, which Edward did in long, confident strides and Elizabeth did in small, teetering steps.

The two visitors were led down the stairs and through a long, narrow portrait gallery. Instead of displaying portraits of royal ancestors, as was the custom in most castles, this gallery featured full-length paintings of the same beautiful woman in many different silver outfits.

"She certainly is beautiful. One might even say 'flawless,'" said Elizabeth.

Edward looked with an artist's eye at the golden hair, the up-turned nose, the almond-shaped eyes and alabaster skin. "Her features are lovely, it's true, but something is missing from each painting."

° veracity: truth

"Well, I think they are perfect." Elizabeth craned her neck to get a better view. The garb in each painting was exquisite, as were the lady's jewels and coiffures°, but nothing compared to the lady's own beauty. This was not the time, however, to gawk and ponder°. Elizabeth was trailing behind Edward and their escort, and she scurried to catch up while stealing a final glimpse of the paintings.

Her gaze continued to be drawn upward as she entered the next room which appeared to be a more traditional portrait gallery. Here, lining the walls, were full-sized renderings of elegant men and women, all dressed in sumptuous° silver garments. Elizabeth was studying the portrait of a man with a silver mustache when he sud-

denly sneezed. Elizabeth stifled a scream. Then she looked around more carefully and realized that all the "portraits" were actually tilted mirrors reflecting the courtiers assembled in the room. Each courtier was so transfixed° by his or her own reflection that no one moved or spoke.

The silence was broken by the footman who rang a small, silver bell. The tinkling was not very loud, but it immediately brought the immobile° crowd to life. Everyone turned to face the silver curtains at the far end of the room, although

° coiffures: hair styles
° gawk and ponder: stare and contemplate
° sumptuous: luxurious, lavish
° transfixed: spellbound, engrossed
° immobile: motionless

many gave last minute glances at the mirrors, followed by rapid adjustments to hair and garments. When all eyes were steadfastly fixed on the same point, the curtains were drawn back. The woman from the

portrait gallery walked through, or rather glided through, for she seemed to walk on air. The crowd murmured justifiable "Oohs" and "Ahhs" at the spectacular sight. Her hair, garments and jewels were so elaborate that they made Elizabeth's elegant outfit appear plain.

The footman announced, unnecessarily, "Princess Flawless," and the courtiers moved into a line while the princess seated herself on a large, silver throne. Edward and Elizabeth looked at each other, shrugged, and joined the end of the line.

The first courtier, an elderly man with a silver goatee, bowed to the princess. "May I say, your Highness, that you look as fresh as the morning dew?"

"You may," she replied in a hushed voice, with a slight nod of her head.

The next courtier, a young woman with black hair tied back in a silver net, said,

"Today you are as radiant° as the sun."

"I know you will enjoy basking in my glow," responded Flawless.

A young man, who looked quite nervous, followed, saying, "Your skin is as smooth as a baby's bottom."

Everyone gasped, and the princess began to fan herself. The young man turned whiter under his powder and stammered, "I mean, as smooth as, as…silk." Everyone breathed a sigh of relief.

The line moved quickly as each courtier heaped trite° praise on the princess. When Elizabeth found herself at the head of the line, she was at a loss. Every standard compliment seemed to have been used. The princess had lips as red as roses, eyes as blue as cornflowers, hair as yellow as daffodils. She was as delicate as a butterfly, as bright as the evening star, and as light as a feather.

Elizabeth offered tentatively, "You are as pretty as a picture," but when an uneasy silence followed, she added, "Well, at least as pretty as the pictures in the gallery." This statement seemed to please the princess, who liked her own animate beauty compared to her inanimate beauty. With sudden clarity, Edward knew what was wrong with all the gallery portraits: there was no life in them, no expression, no emotion. And the problem also existed in the breathing incarnation° of the portraits' subject.

Now it was Edward's turn to speak. He struggled to remember a compliment and blurted out, "You are as toothsome as spun sugar." There was a pause, and then the princess smiled imperceptibly°. It was so slight a movement at the corners of her mouth that Edward thought perhaps he was mistaken.

Princess Flawless spoke in her hushed tones, barely moving her mouth: "Thank you for your unusual compliment. Now, I expect you to turn around."

° radiant: glowing, beaming
° trite: stale, hackneyed
° incarnation: embodiment, living form
° imperceptibly: faintly, barely

The way Flawless said, "I expect," clearly implied, "I command," so Edward did as he was told.

Flawless commented, "It's a good thing you are clever since you are not much to look at. Your ears are quite tolerable, but the rest of you needs improvement." She moved her hand slightly in Elizabeth's direction. "I expect to get a look at you."

Elizabeth moved to the center and turned around. Flawless said with surprising animation, "Ah, what eyes, what skin, what teeth, what hair. Yes, absolute perfection."

Elizabeth blushed and said, "Thank you."

"Oh, I wasn't speaking about you," replied Flawless. "I couldn't help seeing myself in that mirror on the wall." She pointed to a glass over Elizabeth's shoulder. "But I will steel° myself now and look at you." She reluctantly tore her gaze from her own reflection and fixed it on Elizabeth, "Well, your eyebrows are rather acceptable, but you, too, need work."

Edward was about to laugh, but he saw that Elizabeth was about to cry.

"Do not fret, my dear," said Flawless. "You have come to the right place for improvement. I expect that in no time you will be...breathtaking."

Elizabeth smiled with relief, and Edward chided himself for withholding his proper praise of her in the hall. He wished Elizabeth knew that she needed no additional effort to be breathtaking.

Flawless gracefully rose from her throne and limply held out her hand to Edward. "As a reward for winning at competitive compliments, you may escort me to the table. I hope you will not be overwhelmed by the attention my reflected beauty will bestow upon you." Edward had no choice but to take her arm and be scrutinized° as they moved across the floor to the dining room. All the courtiers paired up and followed.

° steel: brace, strengthen, harden
° scrutinized: examined closely, inspected

The dining table shone brightly with sterling pieces. Edward was seated to the right of Flawless, Elizabeth to the left. Flawless directed most of her comments to Elizabeth, in whom she found a more sympathetic, responsive audience. Edward caught snippets of Flawless' monotone° monologue°.

"I know it seems conceited to state that I am the most beautiful woman on earth, but I feel compelled to speak the truth…. Perfection is a heavy burden, but for the enjoyment of mankind, I must preserve and present my gifts…. Of course, I don't like being gawked at all day, but I mustn't deprive others of their joy." During her musings, courtiers would interrupt to compliment Flawless on her hair, her dress, and her jewels, and to share their latest beauty secrets. Everyone moved slowly, spoke quietly, and showed little expression. No one ate much. They were too distracted by their reflections in the gleaming dishes and utensils; knife blades and spoon backs were particularly popular for face checks.

Edward overheard Elizabeth say, "I will definitely try lemon juice on my freckles, olive oil on my chaffed elbows, and cucumbers on my puffy eyes."

Edward interrupted, "And if the treatments fail, at least you'll have the fixings for an excellent salad."

Elizabeth smiled at him.

"Stop that, at once," growled Flawless.

"Stop what?" asked Elizabeth.

"Smiling. It distorts the proper arrangement of the facial features, and worse…" Flawless dropped her voice even lower, hating to utter the words: "It causes wrinkles."

"Oh, I never thought of that," said Elizabeth.

"Why do you think we are so careful about how we speak? Any use of the facial muscles opens the door to unsightly lines. You are forewarned. I expect you will not squander° the meager° gifts of looks you have received. And now, it is time to prepare for this evening's

° monotone: single tone
° monologue: a long speech given by one person
° squander: waste, throw away
° meager: scanty, skimpy

activities. I must go, for there's much to do. I expect to see you there. I am sorry you missed this morning's audience—I was truly resplendent[o] —but I shall be equally dazzling at the ball tonight and there's always tomorrow. And please, for my sake if not your own, expend some effort on your appearance." With that, Flawless handed Elizabeth and Edward a silver sheet of paper with silver writing, and glided out of the room followed by all her courtiers.

Edward looked at the printed sheet. Across the top, in scrolly letters, was the legend, *"Let no one leave Vanitonia...unattractive.* Below, it read as follows:

Daily Duties
May 23

Wake Up	Preliminary primping
Breakfast	Vigorous veneration and ecstatic esteem
	Gratuitous grooming
Luncheon	Ardent admiration and dogged devotion
	Rigorous relaxation
Midday Fete	Competitive compliments and fervent fawning
	Dramatic dressing
Ball	Profuse praise and lavish lauding
Bedtime	Restorative repose

Daily Duties
May 24

Wake Up	Refined readying
Breakfast	Applied approval and accelerated acclamation
	Mandatory make-up

Edward stopped reading and said, "Elizabeth, we've got to get out of this place. Let's change into our clothes and get back on the road."

---

[o] resplendent: shining brightly

"Why? So we can sleep in discomfort for another night? The sun is already setting. Let's spend the night here and get a fresh start in the morning. I expect to enjoy a little 'restorative repose.'"

Edward noticed that Elizabeth was speaking quietly and that her mouth barely moved. "I don't think it's a good idea."

"I let you stay in Energia when you wanted to play," Elizabeth said. "I let you stay in Gluttonia when you wanted to eat. I expect a little indulgence when I want something." She softened her tone. "Besides, if we left, we would miss an opportunity to dance together again."

"If I recall correctly, the reviews of our last efforts were less than favorable," said Edward, but he secretly longed to hold Elizabeth in his arms while flying through space.

"We have an obligation to attend. After all, Princess Flawless is expecting us."

"And how could we resist her winning ways?" responded Edward, capitulating. Despite her best efforts, Elizabeth could not contain a smile.

"If you think you won't be overwhelmed by my reflected beauty, I shall allow you to escort me to my dressing chamber." Elizabeth offered her arm.

Edward took it. "I may never recover, but it shall be worth the sacrifice."

❧❧❧

Hours were spent on dressing for the ball, and Edward arrived long before Elizabeth. When she finally entered, she was more beautiful and elegant than in the afternoon, but she moved even more slowly and carefully. Courtiers thronged° about her, and Edward could not get near. It did not matter much, though, because no one was dancing. While Edward was waiting, he had invited the dark haired girl to dance. She had declined, explaining that she did not want to muss° her hair or dress. Edward assumed everyone harbored

° thronged: swarmed, crowded
° muss: rumple, make messy

that fear, for no one ventured onto the dance floor. No one ate much at the dinner, either. Clearly, the ball was just an excuse to dress up.

Edward left the party early and refused to try on the four different nightshirts the royal tailor proffered. Edward grabbed the closest one and fiercely bid his attendants good night.

In the morning, Edward arose and happily found himself without any attendants. He donned his freshly laundered travel clothes, gathered his bag, and headed to Elizabeth's room. He was pleased to see that Elizabeth also was awake and alone, but concerned that she was seated at a vanity wearing a silver dressing gown and diamond jewelry. She was staring so intently at her own reflection that she did not hear Edward enter. She started when he cleared his throat and said, "Imagine, the belle of the ball is a girl whose sole allurement° is acceptable eyebrows."

"Oh, Edward, do you think they are acceptable?" She kept her eyes glued to the mirror and spoke in a weird, breathy voice.

Edward was surprised by her brazen° appeal for a compliment, but he thought he would humor her. "Of course, they are, Elizabeth. Now could you and your acceptable eyebrows get dressed?"

Just then, the pert maid stepped into the room. "Good mornin', duckies. Today's breakfast gatherin' has been canceled, it has. The poor princess woke up with black circles under her eyes and refuses to see anyone. All the attendants have been called to an emergency meetin'. They're doin' their best to help until the eye expert arrives. The princess expects that you'll use your time wisely and will begin undertakin' all necessary improvements." Having finished her speech, the maid curtsied and withdrew.

"This is great news. Not that I want the princess to suffer, but now I'll have time for all my preparations," said Elizabeth.

° allurement: attraction, charm
° brazen: bold, brash

"The only preparations necessary right now are for you to throw on your dress, grab your bag, and head for Engravia. Or did you forget that we have a mission to accomplish in two and a half days?"

"Don't worry, Edward. I'll get dressed soon enough. Just let me follow a few of the lessons I learned last night while they're fresh in my mind." She reached for a lemon and dabbed the juice on a small freckle on her nose. "I can't believe how I neglected myself on the road. I have three new freckles from the sun and my hands are all rough from the wheelbarrow," she said, reaching for a silver jar of cream.

Edward sighed and took out his ball to pass the time.

"Edward, I expect you to put that thing away. It scares me half to death. What would happen if you threw it wildly and it hit me? I could end up with a black eye or a broken nose. I'd be banned from court for ages."

Edward did not discern° any true emotion in her face or tone, but he decided not to argue. He put the ball in his bag and took out his sketchbook.

"Do you think, Edward, that with a lot of hard work I could look pretty?"

"Elizabeth, you already are...." He paused, then mustered° his courage and said, "Beautiful."

"You're only saying that because you want me to stop fussing. You just want to leave."

Edward was getting annoyed. "I certainly do want to leave. You can believe my compliment or not."

"Last night I received a real compliment. Princess Flawless said that my teeth are quite good. Of course, my hair needs a great deal of attention," she sighed, and began pinning her dark locks atop her head. "Do you think anyone will ever tell me I'm as radiant as the sun?"

"You are as radiant as the sun. It's happened. Now can we go?"

"Edward, you know I can't possibly leave until I'm ready. I expect you to be patient." She began powdering her face.

° discern: detect, perceive
° mustered: gathered, collected

"I won't be patient. We must leave this place. Don't you see? You are caught in its spell?"

"La, you are such a worrier today. Princess Flawless warned me never to worry again because," she lowered her voice, "it causes wrinkles." Seeing Edward's expression, she added, "And frowning is even worse. Compose yourself, Edward. I know we must go, eventually, but I want to look perfect before we do."

"If we can't leave until you're perfect, we shall be here forever," he said harshly.

Elizabeth did not respond to the taunt. She had become completely absorbed in her primping. Her gaze was glued to the mirror and her expression showed no trace of emotion.

She looks almost like a statue, thought Edward; then he shuddered as he realized he was glimpsing the future if Elizabeth remained the mirror's thrall°. Clearly, he couldn't reason with her. How could he make her really *see* what was happening? He sat still for a moment, then applied himself more rigorously to his drawing. When he finished, Edward brought the sketch over to Elizabeth, saying, "You should look at this."

She could barely tear her eyes away from her reflection, but a quick glance confirmed that this drawing was worthy of her attention. It was a drawing of her at the mirror.

"How lovely I look," she said in her breathy voice. "I expect you to draw many portraits of me and I shall hang them in Graycliff for all to enjoy. I am certain I have never looked better."

"Really?" said Edward with disgust. "Perhaps you should look more closely. First, study your portrait from our first evening." He flipped to the page showing Elizabeth laughing in the wind, her eyes full of life and intelligence. "Now look at this." He turned back to the morning's drawing where Elizabeth sat sedate and unemotional.

"But Edward, you have forgotten to put any expression in my eyes. They are blank, empty spaces. I look almost like a corpse."

° thrall: slave, captive

"So you do. Your eyes used to flash and sparkle, now only your jewels do. You have become ugly on the inside while you've beautified the outside," hissed Edward.

The fire in Elizabeth's eyes came back and she glared at Edward. Then, in a wall mirror over Edward's shoulder, Elizabeth caught sight of her grotesque reflection with her powdered face, elaborate hairstyle and angry expression. Instantly, the fire in her eyes was quenched by a flood of tears. "What have I done?" she cried.

While Elizabeth sobbed and blew her nose, Edward gently removed the diamond jewelry and took out the pins from her hair.

When her crying subsided, Edward said, "It's time to put on your old dress."

Elizabeth caught sight of her puffy face with her red, swollen eyes and nose. "Yes, it's the only garment that will suit my current appearance. I just hope nobody sees me on our way out."

"I hope they don't, either, because if they do, they'll throw you into treatments with emergency experts for several days."

Elizabeth smiled weakly at him.

Edward smiled back. "Truly, Elizabeth, I don't think you ever looked lovelier in Vanitonia than right now."

CHAPTER EIGHT

GREEDONIA

Back on the road, Elizabeth continued to sniffle and dab at her eyes with her handkerchief. After she heaved a particularly deep, long sigh, Edward felt compelled to respond.

"I admit that you look absolutely, positively dreadful, but cheer up. It's not permanent, unless, of course, the swelling continues until we turn into stone. Then you'll have bulging eyes and a swollen nose for eternity."

A tear trickled down Elizabeth's face.

Edward teased some more: "If you feel so terrible, there must be some poor hair stylist whose head you can chop off. Or at least you could force him to endure a bad haircut."

The tears left Elizabeth's eyes and were replaced with an angry glare. "Can't you ever be serious? Not everything's a joke."

Edward replied, "Can't you ever be more light-hearted? Not everything's the end of the world. I don't think your diminished° appearance is a matter of high import."

"I was not thinking about that," Elizabeth said more quietly.

"Then why all this profound melancholy°?"

° diminished: lessened, worsened
° profound melancholy: deep sadness

"I'd rather not discuss it," Elizabeth said, her voice shaky with tears again.

"And what if I beg you to tell me?" Edward stopped walking and got down on one knee. "Please, please disclose the awful se-cret that torments you and causes ceaseless moping°. I'm now looking at you with my most earnest, serious expression of com-passion and concern. And remember, you cannot resist my winning ways."

"Oh, fine," said Elizabeth, feeling a bit relieved to unburden her-self. "I'm upset because...because...I am so disappointed in myself. I was greatly in error in my behavior in Vanitonia."

"Is that all that's wrong?" said Edward.

"Could there be anything more wrong? I made a terrible error in judgment and it may have cost us the success of our mission."

"But everyone makes mistakes."

"I do not. Or at least, I never did until this journey. I could for-give myself the sleeping episode in Slothonia, for I was not in possession of my faculties°, but in Vanitonia I was fully cognizant° of my actions and still I persisted° in dallying."

"I can't imagine what you think of my behavior in Energia and Gluttonia," said Edward.

"I expected *you* to make mistakes and assumed I would rescue you. I never thought *I* would need to be rescued." Her voice broke off in a sob.

"Elizabeth, welcome to the human race. We all need to assist others and we all need to be assisted."

"But my need for assistance threatened such dire° consequences. I may have ruined our chances to get to Engravia and back in time. We've already spent three days on the road and we haven't reached

° moping: brooding, pining
° faculties: abilities, powers
° cognizant: conscious, aware
° persisted: continued steadfastly
° dire: dreadful, disastrous

our destination. Don't forget we'll need time to return to the stone and alter it."

"I agree that we've lost a lot of time along the way, but do not despair. We've come such a long distance and what evils can possibly befall us? We've survived the charms of repose, athlethic competition, fine dining, and sartorial° splendor. Surely we have exhausted all the temptations of the journey, and the road to Engravia will be straight, clear, and easy."

Unfortunately, just as Edward uttered his last sentence, the travelers reached an unmarked fork in the path.

"Which way do we go?" asked Elizabeth.

"I have no idea. We had better consult the map."

Elizabeth removed the worn document from her bag, and they both peered at it. They were pleased to see that Engravia was not far, but dismayed that the intersection in question was obliterated° by a dark stain in the parchment. No answer was forthcoming from their perusal°, and they could not afford to wander in the wrong direction. Then Edward noticed on the map that another village, "Greedonia," was very close. When he looked up from the document, he spied the gates off to the right at the bottom of a small hill.

"Look, Elizabeth, there's Greedonia. Unless you have fierce objections to seeking the assistance of others, I suggest we go ask for directions," said Edward, and he headed toward the village. Elizabeth quickly followed.

When they reached the gates, they saw a sign in curly, tarnished gold letters which must have read "Greedonia," but it was so weatherworn as to be illegible°.

° sartorial: pertaining to tailors and clothing
° obliterated: wiped out, erased
° perusal: examination, scrutiny
° illegible: unreadable

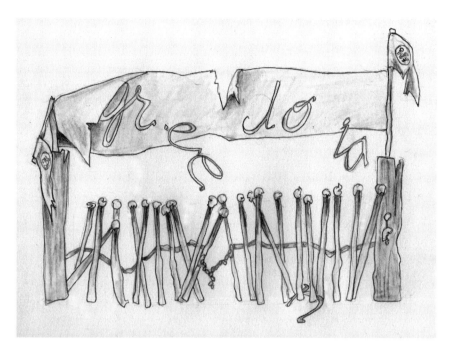

Inside the gates, disrepair reigned. Although everything was once golden, now it was dull and tarnished. Even the bell which Edward tried to ring did not function. Since no one was visible, Edward was reduced to calling loudly, "Good day. Is anybody there?"

Fortunately, someone heard him, for soon a little old man shuffled down the main path. He was dressed in a tattered°, dirty gold tunic and torn gold tights. His golden hair was laced with gray, so it, too, looked tarnished. Elizabeth thought that even the shabbiest beggar in Graycliff would not suffer to be so threadbare, but she was pleased to see help in any form.

The old man pushed open the gate which creaked loudly. "Won't you come in?" asked the old man in a voice as creaky as the gate.

"No, thank you," said Edward, determined to stay on the road. "We stopped merely for assistance. We are on our way to Engravia to hire the Engraver and we are uncertain which road to take."

° tattered: torn, ragged

94

"Engravia," creaked the man. "Why, that road yonder is the way." He pointed to the left side of the fork.

"We are much obliged," said Edward, about to turn back.

"But I wonder what you have brought with you to pay the En-graver," added the old man. "I see no trunks filled with gold, no caskets of jewels. Everyone knows that the Engraver is quite expensive and expects half payment up front."

"Of the expense, we are well aware and, for the expense, we are well prepared," said Elizabeth smugly°. She smiled at Edward and glanced at his belt, then her eyes grew big in horror. "Edward, where is the money bag?"

Edward put his hand down to pat the pouch, and felt nothing. He had a vision of himself in Vanitonia removing the coin bag before his bath....

He clapped his hand to his forehead, "Oh no! I left the coins in Vanitonia." Elizabeth just stood mute. Edward begged her, "Please say something. I believe the proper response is unmitigated gloating°."

Elizabeth remained silent. The old man broke in, in his grating voice, "I'm sure you could engage the Engraver with a mere fifty duc-ats. Perhaps even forty if you're good negotiators."

"It doesn't matter if two ducats would do. We have no money," replied the dejected° Edward.

"Now don't despair," said the old man. "There's work here for you and the missus, and you'll be well-paid for it."

Edward felt a glimmer of hope. "Your offer is very tempting, but we need to confer." He turned to Elizabeth and whispered, "What do you think, 'Wife?'"

"I think I'm not your wife and, thank goodness, never shall be."

"I was asking what you thought about staying to earn back the money we need," said Edward.

° smugly: with self-satisfaction, complacently
° unmitigated gloating: unchecked smug satisfaction
° dejected: sad, down-hearted

"We really can't afford the time," said Elizabeth.

"True, but we also can't afford our poverty. It would be terrible to reach Engravia, only to be turned away for lack of funds. I feel wretched° about my mistake; please give me a chance to make amends°. We still have two and a half days left, and if we hadn't been waylaid so often, I think we could have made the trip in about a day."

Elizabeth thought for a moment. "If you think we can earn the money quickly and get right back on the road, I guess we should go in."

Edward turned to the old man and said, "We have decided to work."

"Good," creaked the old man. "Follow me." He picked up the two traveling bags in his thin arms. He studied Elizabeth's tapestry bag. "This looks like domestic cloth. Probably cost you three ducats. Imported tapestry costs a bit more—four, maybe five ducats—but it's worth the expense. Much nicer than what you've got."

Elizabeth felt mildly insulted, fairly annoyed, and very impatient. "I'll remember to buy the imported cloth next time I need a traveling bag. Now, do you think we could get moving?" The old man obliged and began walking slowly in the direction of the castle.

Along the main path were crumbling stations of gold leaf tables surmounted° by corroded, golden balance scales and abacuses. Elizabeth assumed that this street was once a bustling center of commerce, but now it lay deserted and ruined. As they walked, the old man gloried in his role as tour guide, pointing out with pride various gilded objects from dilapidated° statues to dried up fountains, in each case stating their original purchase price and their current market value.

° wretched: miserable, desolate
° amends: reparation, compensation
° surmounted: topped
° dilapidated: rundown, decrepit

The inside of the castle showed equal signs of faded glory. Golden sunlight flooded through the windows, exposing the flaws of the frayed gold carpet, peeling gold leaf furniture, and numerous cobwebs. All the furnishings provided fresh fodder° for the old man's commentary on original expense and current prices.

Elizabeth assumed that no woman would consent to live with such decay and disorder and, hoping to change the subject, inquired, "Is Greedonia ruled by a king?"

All she got was a "Yes," and a hasty return to a discourse on the cost of the disintegrating° gold drapes.

After passing through the shabby anteroom°, the three arrived at the throne room which was crowded with broken tables, propped up against the walls, each sagging under dusty piles of gold coins. Elizabeth wondered why, with such wealth abounding°, Greedonia should be so rundown.

The old man put down the bags and looked at Edward expectantly, his palm outstretched. Edward dug deep into his tunic pocket and found a thin, worn copper penny. Edward handed the coin to the old man, whose eyes brightened as he polished the coin on his ragged clothes and slipped it carefully into his pocket.

"Please, we'd like to see the king now," said Edward.

"You may," answered the old man, but he remained stationary°.

"Could we do so promptly? We're in quite a rush," said Elizabeth.

"Immediately," said the old man, still immobile.

"Perhaps we haven't been clear. We want to speak with the king. He's the fellow who wears the crown," said Edward.

"Oh, of course, wait just a minute," and the old man shuffled out the door into a chamber behind the throne room.

As soon as he was gone, Elizabeth whispered, "How very vexing° that the old servant is so slow, both physically and mentally."

° fodder: fuel, material
° disintegrating: crumbling, decomposing
° anteroom: foyer, front hall
° abounding: in full supply, teeming
° stationary: motionless
° vexing: annoying, bothersome

"He does seem on his last legs. Can you imagine when he gets to the Pearly Gates? He'll be telling everyone, 'Those Gates cost 89,632 ducats originally and now they are worth twice as much,'" said Edward.

"And he'll probably urge all the angels to melt down their halos to trade in the gold."

Their musings were interrupted by a good deal of clanging and banging in the next room. They heard the creaky voice saying with concern, "Where, oh where...? If only I knew." Edward and Elizabeth feared the king was playing a strange game of hide-and-seek with his servant. Finally, they heard a triumphant "Aha!" and the sound of slow footsteps.

When the old man emerged he was wearing a cracked, bent crown and a moth-eaten, stained robe.

"I must thank you for the reminder about my crown. I have so few visitors that I forget to don my royal attire," he said.

"Then you are the king?" asked Edward, astonished.

"King Pointless of Greedonia," he answered, bowing. "At your service."

"Sire, as you know, we would like to be at *your* service." Edward returned the bow.

"And so you shall be, for there's much work to be done," creaked Pointless, gesturing about the messy room with a broad sweep of his arm.

Elizabeth figured if she could push a wheelbarrow, she could do housework. "I can sweep and dust, while Edward mops, scrubs and polishes."

"Why would we waste precious time doing that?" asked Pointless. "I have real, important work for you to do: I want you to help me count my money."

Edward looked around the room at the massive piles of gold and boasted, "I can already tell you how much you have."

"Really?" said Pointless eagerly.

"A lot!" declared Edward.

Pointless looked disappointed. "I want to know the exact amount right down to the last penny," he said and tapped his pocket where his tip was safely stored.

"But why do you need exactitude°? It will take so long to count all these coins, and I can't imagine you could spend them all in one life-time," said Elizabeth.

"That's where you're mistaken, my dear. I have plans. Lots of plans. I like to think big. Very big. Imagine this castle rebuilt to twice its current size, filled with solid gold furniture, draperies made of spun gold thread, thick golden carpets, and a staff of hundreds to preserve its perfection."

"It does sound lovely...and expensive," said Elizabeth.

"But then, I wonder, is 'twice as big' large enough? Why not thrice° as big? And shouldn't the road leading to the castle be paved in gold? And what of my personal wardrobe? To fit in with my lush surroundings, shouldn't I wear fabrics from across the world: fine damasks, brocades, satins? I will have to entertain foreign dignitaries

° exactitude: precision, accuracy
° thrice: three times

and royals in the highest fashion. They shall be served the rarest morsels from gold vessels on to gold plates to be eaten with gold utensils. Even the food will be decorated with 24 karat gold leaf!" His eyes gleamed with excitement at the prospect of the future. He continued, "Of course, I shall have other expenses. I want to see the world. I shall travel the seas in a golden ship and the roads in a golden carriage. I shall bring an entourage° of many servants and companions to ease the burden of travel and enliven the journey. I shall present to foreign rulers costly gifts of exotic spices, fragrant perfumes, and beautiful jewels. Ah, the future is bright and the options are endless, but I must know how much I can spend before I make any commitments."

Elizabeth was not convinced. "Wouldn't it make sense to spend some of your vast fortune to preserve what you already own?"

"Nonsense, why waste money on things from my past? No, I want to save it all to put toward my future."

Edward was entranced. "We're certainly glad to be of assistance in such a noble and important endeavor. Where do we begin?"

"I'm so glad you asked. I can't wait to get you started." Pointless led each of them to a sagging table. "Please count the coins from your table's pile. For every thousand coins you count, you are entitled to one coin for yourself. I think you'll find those terms fair."

"More than fair. Downright generous," said Edward as he dove into his pile. He counted off by twos, setting off groups of ten, and when he had ten tens, he pushed the stacks aside, then he repeated the procedure until he had ten of the hundred groups, and finally, he set one coin out for himself. He became completely absorbed in his task, and was counting as fast as he could. Elizabeth tried to apply herself, wanting to amass° the forty coins as soon as possible. Time evaporated with the painstaking work.

° entourage: group of staff and followers
° amass: accumulate, accrue

Pointless, who was working at a table across the room, abruptly got up and declared, "It's time to eat. We can't work on empty stomachs; we might make a mistake and even one coin's miscalculation could lead to disaster. What if I thought I could afford everything I set my heart on, only to find I was one ducat short? I shall return momentarily with some refreshment." He shuffled out of the room.

Once he was gone, Elizabeth looked at her pile of twelve coins. She checked on Edward who had fourteen.

"Edward, we have twenty-six coins all together. I think that's enough to show the Engraver that we are honest and mean to pay."

"It's not nearly enough. Not only do we have to pay the Engraver, but we have to start thinking more clearly about this quest. We've been approaching it all wrong. We set out with no plan, no assistance. We should hire others to help us."

"But according to the map, we're almost there," argued Elizabeth.

"Well, I would feel much better if we hired a guide who knew the fastest route. What could it cost? Five, six ducats? It would be money well spent. And I'm sure you're getting tired. We could hire four young men to carry us in sedan chairs on their shoulders."

"I don't want to be carried."

"At least we should hire some protection, now that we have money with us. Just two or three armed guards to ward off highway robbers."

"I'll take my chances."

"Elizabeth, you need to learn to think big."

"I can think big: we'll hire two elephants to carry us on their backs," Elizabeth said.

"I hadn't thought of that. I was considering black stallions, but elephants would be more interesting," Edward said earnestly.

"And would take months to procure...months we do not have."

"Elizabeth, with enough money we can move mountains."

"We don't need to move mountains, we just need to alter one large stone."

Pointless returned, carrying three small bowls of thin gruel and three cups of tepid water. Pointless apologized perfunctorily°, explaining that he had released all his servants until his money was counted and his plans were firm. They all ate quickly and went back to work. Edward continued counting rapidly. Elizabeth tried to get his attention, but he steadfastly avoided any eye contact.

Elizabeth felt her eyelids growing heavy with fatigue from the last night's revels° and from the day's tedium°. She closed her eyes and dozed.

When she awoke, the sun had set and the room glowed with the golden light of candles. Edward was still working at a furious pace. She knew they were stranded in the castle until daybreak, but refused to do any more counting. Edward's pile was more than large enough to engage the Engraver, and she saw no reason to do more. She read her book a little, scribbled a bit, urged Edward to get some rest, and then went to the front hall to a broken bench for a good night's rest. She used her bag as a pillow and wondered if a more expensive, imported bag would have been more comfortable.

ঙঝঙঝঙঝ

The first rays of sunlight woke Elizabeth. She got up and headed across the foyer toward the throne room. A large, golden book on a gilt bookstand caught her eye. She went over to it. The book, whose spine was broken and pages ripped, bore the title, "The Accounts of Greedonia." Not exactly pleasure reading, but Elizabeth could not resist a quick look. All the writing was in gold ink on pale gold paper and the first page bore the legend, *"Let no one leave Greedonia...poor."*

° perfunctorily: with little interest, superficially
° revels: festivities, partying
° tedium: boredom, dullness

As Elizabeth flipped through the pages, she noticed that the early entries were in the scrawly, loose hand of a child, the middle entries were in the bolder hand of an adult, and the most recent entries were a reversion° to the scrawly hand. On closer inspection, Elizabeth saw that all the entries had been made by one person, King Pointless, over the course of his life. The early entries showed the many expenses of a monarch, but over time the expenses had grown smaller and smaller until they had completely disappeared. The entries also enumerated° holdings of wealth, with little notations in the margins like "Can now afford gold surfaced pool," and "Add golden chariot to list," and "Ready for new gold velvet robe."

At the top of each page, including the new page for today, May 25th, Pointless had written:

Today's tasks:
Morning: *count coins*
Noon: *count coins*
Night: *count coins*

Elizabeth realized that Pointless had been counting his coins and making his plans all day, every day since he was a child. His accounting was the work of an entire lifetime, and he had not fulfilled a single dream.

She knew she had to get Edward out of Greedonia. She grabbed her bag and ran to the throne room. Both Edward and Pointless had fallen asleep on top of their piles of coins. Elizabeth shook Edward. As soon as he opened his eyes and sat up, he began counting again.

"Edward, we must leave this place. You've earned plenty of coins for our journey."

"Who's thinking about only our journey? Once it's over, I'll have my whole life ahead of me, and with the fortune I'm amassing, I'll be able to afford anything." Clearly, as Edward's pile had grown, so had

° reversion: return
° enumerated: specified, set forth

his plans. "I shall have the most luxurious castle, the most elegant clothes, the finest food, the most entertaining performers..."

Elizabeth interrupted, "But you already have all that, within reason. You want for nothing. What good are a hundred tunics in your closet when you can wear only one on your back?"

Edward looked at her indulgently and said, "You've just got to learn to think big. Now please be quiet so I can count. I need to be clear-headed and composed to do this right."

Elizabeth grabbed his arm. "Please, Edward, we've got to get on the road immediately. We only have one and a half days to get to Engravia and back."

Edward pulled his arm back gently. He seemed oddly detached. "Just give me a few more minutes, then."

Elizabeth replied angrily, "No, we've got to leave now." She slammed her fist on the wobbly table which immediately collapsed, sending all the coins—counted and uncounted—flying. To make matters worse, the falling table knocked into Elizabeth's table which in turn hit the next table and the next, till all the tables around the room fell like dominoes. Coins lay everywhere. Miraculously, Pointless slid to the floor and slept through the whole disaster. In fact, he looked quite comfortable lying in a pile of his beloved coins.

"Oh dear," was all that Elizabeth could think to say. She steeled herself for Edward's wrath. Instead, he sat down on the floor and calmly began counting again.

"What are you doing?" Elizabeth demanded.

"I'm resuming my counting. I'm sure you understand that I must earn back the forty ducats we need," replied Edward.

"Are you crazy? Time is much more precious now than those coins. We'll just have to get the Engraver to trust us. You can be very persuasive when you want to be."

"Elizabeth, calm down. I am not budging until I've regained the necessary funds."

Elizabeth was desperate; time was running out and once again Edward was unmovable. Obviously, physical force had accomplished nothing. It occurred to her that sometimes, when actions fail, words succeed. She ran to her bag and grabbed her book. Turning to her writing from the previous night, she read aloud to Edward:

"What care I for diamonds
When stars are twinkling high?
And what care I for sapphires?
There's the deep blue summer sky."

Edward stopped counting and rubbed his chin.

"What care I for rubies
When the fire's glowing red?
What use have I for emeralds
When I make the grass my bed?"

Edward cracked his knuckles and scratched his back.

"What care I for perfumes
When flowers scent the air?
What use have I for rare silk fans
When the breeze is in my hair?"

Edward stretched out his arms and flexed his fingers.

"What care I for fine wines
When there's water cool and clear?
What use have I for heavy furs
When my true love's arms are near?"

Edward squirmed, and wriggled, and twitched.

"Yes, what care I for riches
When, as it's widely known,
They can't buy Nature's beauty
Or undo what's set in stone."

As Elizabeth finished, Edward jumped up from the floor. What a boon° that Edward had disclosed that poetry made him irritable and fidgety. Elizabeth never knew if it was the mere reading of poetry that broke his composure° or the sentiment the poem expressed, but Edward grabbed his bag and said, "Let's get out of here."

While passing through the creaky front gate, Edward mused, "We're probably the only people who have ever left Greedonia poorer than we arrived."

"But, Edward, we came with no money and left with no money."

"You forget the tip I gave King Pointless," said Edward.

"Well, look at the advantage we gained," urged Elizabeth. "We won't have to fear the attacks of highway robbers."

° boon: blessing, godsend
° composure: serenity, calmness

CHAPTER NINE

UTOPIA: PART I

Edward and Elizabeth had followed the "road yonder" for about two hours when they saw a village surrounded by a high wall carved out of solid stone. They could not actually see the village, just the wall, but its size suggested that a village lay within. Above what they judged to be the entrance—there were lines cut in the stone the size to admit a person—was chiseled the word ENGRAVIA. A heavy iron knocker was attached nearby.

Edward and Elizabeth ran toward the wall. Edward grabbed Elizabeth's hands and they spun around, laughing. "I wish I could do cartwheels and back flips like Prince Restless," said Edward. "They seem required at the moment."

"Perhaps a few words on this historic occasion would be fitting," said Elizabeth. "I think the best way to express our triumphant arrival is to say, with great solemnity° and profundity°: HURRAY!"

Her shout caught the attention of two figures seated near the wall in the shade of a large tree. They moved closer, but went unnoticed by Edward and Elizabeth.

Edward said, "And now that you so ably declared our sentiments to the world, would you like the honor of knocking?"

"I don't think I need to knock. My heart is pounding so hard that the inhabitants of Engravia should hear it through their wall."

"Let's not take any chances. We'll use the knocker, just to be sure." Edward moved toward the iron ring.

"Wait!" cried Elizabeth, turning serious. She grabbed Edward's arm. "We need to decide what we're going to tell the Engraver."

"That's simple. We'll explain that the stone was engraved to require our marriage, that we cannot spend our lives together, and that we need the enchantment undone," replied Edward.

"I don't know if that's the proper approach. Lady Claire said she had never heard of an engraving being altered. The Engraver might refuse to come with us and our journey would be futile°. Maybe we should say that we have a job and ask the stonecutter to join us. Once we get to the stone, I cannot imagine we would be refused help."

"I don't feel comfortable with being deceptive°."

"It's not being deceptive. It's telling the truth...up to a point," argued Elizabeth.

"Well, I believe in telling the whole truth," declared Edward.

° solemnity: gravity, seriousness
° profundity: insight, depth of understanding
° futile: in vain, useless
° deceptive: misleading, deceitful

"And I believe in negotiating with tact. We only have a day and a half to accomplish our goal. After midnight tomorrow, you won't be telling any stories, whole or partial, if we don't succeed."

"Then you won't be telling any lies."

"I am not lying. You just don't understand the subtleties° of the situation. I think I am more capable of making this decision," asserted Elizabeth.

"I resent the implication° that I'm not capable of sound, reasoned judgment. I may not be as bookish as you, but I possess much more common sense."

"How can you say that? Look at your behavior in Energia, Gluttonia, and Greedonia."

"Greedonia was not a mistake. I was working hard to earn back the money we sorely needed. With a self-indulgent slam of your fist, you frittered° away hours of work," said Edward.

"If I hadn't acted in Greedonia, we'd still be there. Your mistakes caused three critical delays along the way. We have only a day and a half left and, thanks to you, we probably will never complete this mission. The statue of the great Prince Edward of Whitehill will bear the inscription, 'He was a competitive, greedy hog.'"

"Well, the statue of the Princess Elizabeth of Graycliff will read, 'She was a lazy, vain sneak.' Let's not forget that you invaded my privacy. Nor that you made two major mistakes which caused delays."

"I already told you, I don't count Slothonia," said Elizabeth.

"That's a distinction worthy of Sir Robert. A clever construct to make yourself feel better. I managed to rouse myself in Slothonia, but you didn't. I think your inability to admit to your mistakes is just another major character flaw," he said.

"Don't invite me to examine all your character flaws or we'll be standing here until we turn to marble."

° subtleties: nuances, fine points
° implication: inference, suggestion
° frittered: wasted, squandered

The two faced each other, locked in battle like the wrestlers of Energia, hurling insults and recriminations°. Each was so intent on proving the other inferior, that they were oblivious° to the approach from behind of the two figures. One figure tapped Elizabeth's shoulder while the other tapped Edward's. Both Elizabeth and Edward jumped with fright and spun around. Their fright immediately turned to astonishment, for Elizabeth found herself staring into the face of a handsome young man with wavy dark hair and serious brown eyes and Edward found himself staring into the face of a beautiful young woman with straight golden hair and amused blue eyes. Both Edward and Elizabeth thought, I must be dreaming, and both were rendered speechless.

The young man broke the silence. "Excuse us," he said in his deep, calm voice, "we could not help but overhear you, and we hoped we could ease your minds regarding a key concern."

"You're very kind," said Elizabeth.

The young woman said, in her teasing, musical voice, "More importantly, we wanted to break up this battle before it turned to fisticuffs°. Although I would have put money on the feisty wench°."

"My jaw appreciates your timely intervention," said Edward.

With quiet formality the young man proceeded. "Please allow us to introduce ourselves. I am Prince Peerless from the fine kingdom of Utopia."

The young woman said lightly, "And I am his sister, Princess Matchless, from the fun kingdom of Utopia."

The two royals gestured across the path to a gray and white castle that stood on a nearby hill overlooking the valley. Elizabeth stared at the castle which reminded her of Graycliff; she felt a sharp pang of

---

° recriminations: accusations, reproaches
° oblivious: unaware of
° fisticuffs: fist fighting
° feisty wench: spirited young woman

homesickness. Edward stared at the castle which reminded him of Whitehill; he felt the same pang.

Prince Peerless said, "We gather, from your animated discussion, that you are Prince Edward and Princess Elizabeth and that you have traveled from your kingdoms to seek the help of the Engraver. We cannot guarantee that your request will be honored; however, we can assure you that you should have sufficient time for your return trip."

Princess Matchless continued, "The Engraver is very wise and knows all the best routes. You could make the return in under twelve hours, unless you take out time for 'animated discussions' and armed combat."

Prince Peerless said, "So we suggest you join us for a brief visit, and when you're calm and collected..."

Princess Matchless interrupted, "And no longer murderous..."

"You'll return to Engravia with your request," finished Peerless.

Elizabeth responded, "What a lovely invitation. It sounds absolutely delightful. But I think that we should take care of our business first, and visit later."

Edward chimed in, "I shudder to agree with Elizabeth, but I fear I must in this case."

Prince Peerless said to Elizabeth, "I fully understand your desire to go, but I insist you reconsider. You'll miss the finals of the poetry competition today. Your reputation as a writer precedes° you, and we need new talent for our anthology°. The publication of your poems would impress all your subjects."

Princess Matchless said to Edward, "I can't comprehend° your need to leave, but I wouldn't dream of imposing my judgment. However, you will miss out on the sailing finals. You have an excellent reputation as a sailor and I desperately need a co-captain on my boat. The trophy would impress all your subjects."

Elizabeth turned to Peerless and asked, "Are you certain the Engraver knows a faster route?"

"On my sacred word of honor," he replied. "Please say you'll stay."

Edward turned to Matchless, "And you're sure we could return in half a day?"

"You can have a midday meal here and be home in time for a midnight morsel," she affirmed. "Please say you'll stay."

"We'll stay!" said Edward and Elizabeth in unison.

The two couples ascended the hill, Elizabeth with Prince Peerless, Edward with Princess Matchless. By the time they reached the top, Elizabeth was impressed by the intelligence and dignity of Peerless; his elegant brown tunic and tights added to his allure by reflecting his dark hair and eyes. Edward was equally taken with Matchless's humor and vivacity°. He even noticed that her simple, fitted dress in sapphire blue perfectly matched her merry eyes.

Over the village gates flew a flag with the motto, "Let no one leave Utopia...unfulfilled." Elizabeth and Edward inquired about the village schedule and were told that numerous cultural and athletic

° precedes: comes before
° anthology: compilation, volume of collected works
° comprehend: understand, grasp
° vivacity: exuberance, liveliness

events occurred every day, but that their hosts wanted the particulars to be a surprise.

Utopia was a welcome contrast to the other villages. It looked normal and familiar to Edward and Elizabeth. What they did not notice, being absorbed in their conversations, was that all the men had blonde hair, blue eyes and wore jewel-toned outfits, and all the women had dark hair, brown eyes and wore earth-toned outfits. The effect, although subtle, was to show both Princess Matchless and Prince Peerless off to best advantage.

As the four strolled down the main street, they marveled at the gardens ablaze with lush, multi-colored flowers. Princess Matchless modestly admitted that she selected the plantings. Upon entering the castle, they admired the luxurious, tasteful furnishings in quiet, muted colors. Prince Peerless proudly proclaimed that he oversaw the decoration.

Matchless whisked away Edward to the lake and the races. With equal speed, Peerless led Elizabeth to the poetry competition. No one had time for even a good-bye.

ε❧ε❧ε❧

Edward was thrilled to be in the sailboat race. The wind was strong, the boat trim°, and the competition fierce. Right down to the finish, the boat Edward and Matchless shared was tied with another. At the last moment, Princess Matchless grabbed the tiller from Edward and steered toward the other boat's flank°. To avoid a collision, the competitors swerved, and Matchless raced across the finish line. Edward was concerned by the unusual tactic, but no one raised any objections. Edward dismissed his reservations when Matchless presented him with a large, shiny trophy to the enthusiastic cheering of the crowd.

° trim: in good order, neat and smart
° flank: side

Elizabeth was equally enchanted to be at the poetry competition. Many fine poets read their works, but only Elizabeth received an ovation which Prince Peerless led. Peerless even insisted that the audience discuss the merits of Elizabeth's writing. Elizabeth was named the best new poet at the competition. At first, she felt guilty that others had not received equal attention, but she dismissed such feelings upon learning that three of her poems would be included in the new anthology°.

The morning had dissolved in these pleasant pastimes, and both Elizabeth and Edward were invited to dine with their respective companions. Peerless brought Elizabeth to the castle's elegant dining hall where they found a sumptuous feast awaiting them. Servants in formal livery° served them delicacies on gold plates. The conversation never lagged as the two discussed literature, music, art and dancing. They found that they agreed on all matters of refined° taste.

Just as they were confirming their mutual devotion to Gregorian chants°, Princess Matchless and Edward burst into the dining hall from the kitchen. Edward was carrying a large basket filled with crusty bread, cheese, pears, gingerbread, and a jug. The princess was carrying a folded blanket. They whispered to one another, laughing.

Edward saw Elizabeth engaged in quiet conversation while she ate a magnificent feast. The leg of mutton looked good, the dining hall chairs comfortable, and Elizabeth happy. He felt a twinge of jealousy, but dismissed it.

Elizabeth saw Edward engaged in an animated exchange on his way to a simple outdoor lunch. The bread and cheese looked good, the beautiful day inviting, and Edward looked happy. She felt a pang of envy, but shrugged it off.

° anthology: compilation, volume of collected works
° livery: uniform
° refined: cultured, sophisticated
° Gregorian chants: church choral music from the early Middle Ages

Soon Edward and Matchless were out of the room, their laughter faintly echoing down the hall.

Prince Peerless cleared his throat. "I cannot imagine why anyone would want to eat al fresco°. I would hate to contend with all those insects."

"I don't know...food tastes better if you share, and ants are always willing to oblige."

"Perhaps," he said without conviction°, "but nothing could make that food taste better. It was barely fit for swine°."

"Then put me in the sty and fill my trough°," declared Elizabeth.

"Excuse me, I don't understand you."

"Never mind," sighed Elizabeth, and she put down her fork.

When the elegant meal was over, Prince Peerless asked Elizabeth to attend an afternoon concert. He observed that Princess Matchless and Edward seemed perfect for one another and should be allowed to run around outdoors, like wild savages. Elizabeth decided that if Edward was having fun, she would, too.

The concert was wonderful, with excellent musicians and singers performing in a gilded music room. The highlight was when Prince Peerless sang love ballads, of his own composing, which he pointedly addressed to Elizabeth. She couldn't help but blush.

〰️〰️〰️

Outside, Edward and Princess Matchless enjoyed a hearty meal, during which they laughed a lot and discovered that they shared a passion for many athletic activities. When they finished, Matchless invited Edward to attend an archery tournament. He hesitated until Matchless pointed out that Prince Peerless and Elizabeth seemed to be unavailable to anyone but each other. Edward decided that if

° al fresco: Italian for "in the open air"
° conviction: certainty
° swine: pigs
° trough: feeding trench

Elizabeth was enjoying herself, so would he. They headed to the tournament.

Although they had intended to go as spectators, Edward and Matchless were drawn into the competition as a team. On his first try, Edward hit a bull's eye. Matchless then aimed at the same target and landed her shot right next to Edward's.

"Look, our arrows are kissing," she teased. Edward blushed.

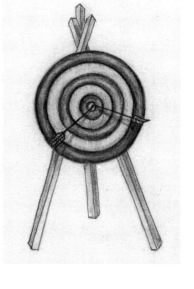

❧❧❧

After the concert, Prince Peerless insisted that Elizabeth visit his private study to view his art collection. He could not draw himself, but he had a well-trained eye and could appreciate virtuosity°. Peerless boasted that his collection contained examples of all the finest artists alive. Elizabeth looked at the drawings against a new standard: Edward's work. Although some of these drawings displayed more technical skill than Edward's, none of them achieved his emotional depth. Elizabeth wanted to tell Peerless that his collection was incomplete, but she held her tongue. It was bad enough that she had unveiled Edward's secret; she would not divulge° it to others.

When the tournament ended, Princess Matchless suggested that they go horseback riding before the sun set. Edward readily agreed, and they ran across the back lawn toward the stables. As he passed the study window, Edward saw Elizabeth bent over a portfolio° of drawings, discussing its contents with Peerless. After a day of

---

° virtuosity: extraordinary skill, talent
° divulge: reveal, disclose
° portfolio: a collection held in a folder

activity outdoors, he longed to be inside quietly resting. The twinge of jealousy returned, and he turned his gaze away.

At that moment, Elizabeth looked out the window and saw Edward running, the wind in his hair, his limbs moving fluidly, Matchless at his side. After a sedentary° day indoors, she longed to be outside stretching her limbs. She felt a pang of envy and forced herself to look back at the portfolio.

Prince Peerless declared that it was time to change for the evening's festivities. With great excitement, he told Elizabeth that he had arranged a ball in her honor. Peerless led Elizabeth to a beautiful, ornate bedroom and left to change his clothes. A lovely brown gown was laid out on the bed; it fit Elizabeth perfectly. Peerless returned in an embroidered tunic, and they went down to the grand ballroom for an evening of light refreshments and courtly dances.

Prince Peerless never left Elizabeth's side and insisted they lead every dance. Elizabeth had to admit he was a superb partner, yet she missed the wild, unrestrained dancing she had experienced with Edward. She found herself searching the crowd for his face, but with no success. After several dances she declared that she was tired; Peerless said that, as the guest of honor and the "only desirable partner," she could not retire so early. She reluctantly agreed to stay.

❧❧❧

After the horseback ride, Matchless invited Edward to a swim. Edward protested that they hadn't proper swimming attire. Matchless just laughed and peeled down to her cotton slip. Edward followed suit, leaving his undergarments on, and they plunged into the lake. The refreshing swim was followed by star-gazing. Matchless suggested that they see who could name the most constellations. Edward wanted to quietly enjoy the sky's beauty, but Matchless kept calling out "Cassiopeia" and "Gemini" and so on. She was well

° sedentary: inactive, sitting-down

prepared for the competition, and won handily. She offered Edward dinner as a consolation prize.

The two hurried to the kitchen to raid the pantry. When they finished, Edward asked Matchless to dance to the music that wafted° in from the ballroom. She refused, dismissing dancing as a hateful activity promoted by shoemakers to increase sales. Disappointed, Edward announced that he got to name the next activity: sleep.

Princess Matchless led Edward to a handsome, simple bedroom. He asked where Elizabeth would lodge and was informed that her room was next door. Once Matchless left, Edward crept to Elizabeth's room, but found it empty. He realized he had not spoken to Elizabeth since they had agreed to visit Utopia, and was surprised that he would care. He laughed at his own folly and put his tired body to bed.

When Elizabeth finally convinced Prince Peerless to allow her to retire, she went up to her room. Through the wall, she heard Edward's familiar snores. She felt sorry that she had not been able to wish him a "good night," then wondered at her own silliness. She crawled into bed and fell asleep.

° wafted: drifted, floated

CHAPTER TEN

UTOPIA: PART II

The next morning, Edward and Elizabeth awoke with great anticipation. Today was May 26th and tonight, at the final stroke of twelve, their fate would be sealed. They both hastily dressed and hurried down to the dining hall for breakfast.

The prince and princess were eagerly awaiting their arrival, each seated at opposite ends of the large table. Prince Peerless jumped up and helped Elizabeth into her seat. Princess Matchless smiled, gestured to the chair nearest her and said, "It's not exactly grass and dirt, but it will have to do."

The liveried servants brought Elizabeth a fluffy herb omelet and some honey cakes and Edward two hard-boiled eggs and a hard roll. Elizabeth looked longingly at Edward's plate; Edward looked longingly at Elizabeth's.

"Do you want to switch?" she asked.

"I was just about to ask you the same question," he replied, smiling.

The servants exchanged the plates, while Peerless and Matchless endeavored to engage their partners in separate conversations.

Peerless said, "Elizabeth, I have saved the most special activity for this morning."

"But, Peerless, you know I must go to Engravia."

"Of course you must. But there is no rush. As long as you leave by midday you will have ample time to make your request and travel back."

"I really think we have tarried too long. I must beg leave to go as soon as breakfast is done," she said.

"Then you will miss the finest treasure in all of Utopia: my library. I have never allowed a beautiful woman to enter, but now I want to share it with *you*."

"I would like to see it," said Elizabeth, not insensible° to the compliment. She tried to catch Edward's eye to ask permission, but he was too busy talking to Matchless. Edward's face was obscured, but Matchless was in full view and Elizabeth observed the expression on the girl's pretty face. It was the same look Edward had given her while they were dancing. It was the look of unrestrained° admiration. Elizabeth feared that Edward was reciprocating° the look, and said loudly, "Yes, of course I'll go with you."

"You have made me the happiest man in Utopia!" Peerless exclaimed.

"Don't worry, you'll get over it," teased Elizabeth. Peerless just looked confused.

At the other end of the table, Princess Matchless and Edward also were discussing plans.

Matchless said, "If you thought yesterday was fun, you were wrong. It was nothing compared to today. I have big plans for us—bigger than the nose on that servant." She pointed to a waiter who had an unusually large proboscis°.

Edward responded, "I'd love to spend more time with you, but I have to get to Engravia."

° insensible: lacking feeling, numb
° unrestrained: unreserved, uninhibited
° reciprocating: returning, interchanging
° proboscis: nose

"There's plenty of sand in the hourglass. Come with me to my favorite spot in all of Utopia, atop a small hill. The company might not be ideal, but the views will be."

"Couldn't we wait until my return as the hero of this dangerous mission?"

"We could, but I'd like to show it this morning to the mere mortal Edward. I've never shared the spot with anyone, but I'll make an exception for you."

Edward hesitated, wanting to confer with Elizabeth. He looked over and, though he could not see her face, saw that she was busy conversing. Edward could see Peerless's face with its look of radiant absorption°. Edward tried to remember when he had last seen that expression: it was the way Elizabeth had looked when she had studied his drawings. He feared that Elizabeth was reciprocating Peerless's look of esteem and, all at once, he felt angry. He turned to Matchless and said, "All right, let's get this tour going." He pretended to be a guide: "The merely scenic is on the right, the truly sublime° is on the left."

❧❧❧

The library lived up to its billing as a major attraction of Utopia. Around its interior, it boasted dark wood shelves that spanned from the floor to the high ceilings, all of them filled with books. Elizabeth smiled with delight.

Prince Peerless said, "I've read every book in here."

Elizabeth was highly impressed. "I'd like to spend enough time here so I could read everything."

Prince Peerless said, "That could easily be arranged. I knew you would appreciate this place."

"I don't appreciate it; I love it!" she said.

° absorption: fascination, interest
° sublime: magnificent, inspiring, awesome

"Well, I guarantee you'll appreci-ate—or even love—this," said Peerless, and he handed her a small wrapped package.

Elizabeth opened it and found an illuminated book that was so rare that she had only heard of it, but never seen it before. As she turned its pages, she discovered ancient poems, songs, and artwork.

"Thank you so much. I've always wanted a copy," she said.

"I knew you would. I will always be able to anticipate your needs and desires."

Elizabeth looked up and asked, "So where are my diamond tiara and ermine cape?"

Peerless looked flustered°. "Those will take a while to procure..."

Elizabeth saw his distress. "It was just a joke."

"Oh, I did not understand. Perhaps you could be more serious because we have important matters to discuss. It cannot have es-caped your notice that I am besotted° with you. I would face mortal danger for you—slay dragons, fight ogres, battle giants..."

Elizabeth interrupted, "Would you even brave clumsy dance partners?"

"How could they be life threatening?" asked Peerless.

"Never mind."

"Anyway, I would like you to consent to be my partner...for your Engravia mission. We could be a good team together, I just know it."

"But what about Edward?" asked Elizabeth. "I promised to travel with him."

___

° flustered: anxious, upset
° besotted: love-struck, smitten

"You only promised to travel *to* Engravia with him; you never said anything about the return."

"A distinction worthy of Sir Robert," said Elizabeth.

"Once again, I fail to comprehend you. But I hope you understand me. You are the woman of my dreams and I demand to help you. Edward is nothing but a boorish° jokester. I don't think he can succeed on this mission, but I could. Consider how he has jeopardized your chances with his weakness."

"He did make mistakes, but...so did I." Elizabeth felt she had to make the admission. "He saved me on two occasions. I would never have gotten here without him."

"You are too easy on him and too hard on yourself. You had to save him three times. He was the greater burden. You owe him nothing. Remember, he thinks you are 'a lazy, vain sneak.'"

Tears sprang to Elizabeth's eyes at the memory of those words.

"Go to Engravia with me and return triumphantly to the stone. Let the people of Graycliff know who is the true hero of this adventure. And please, let it be me, not the unworthy Edward, at your side. I will give you a few minutes to decide." And with that, Peerless left the room.

Elizabeth's head was awhirl with conflicting thoughts and emotions. What should she do? She needed to settle down and think. She looked around the library, hoping to find a calming distraction. Then she spied just what she wanted.

෫🐦෫🐦෫🐦

Princess Matchless showed Edward the view from the hilltop which was a spectacular symphony of colors and textures. Matchless wanted to stay to pick flowers, but Edward insisted they head back to the castle. Matchless agreed, as long as they could race to the bottom of the hill to a sprawling willow tree. Whoever touched the tree first would be the winner and could choose the next activity.

° boorish: rude, coarse

Knowing Matchless could not keep pace with his long legs and wanting the next activity to be packing, Edward assented to the proposal. Matchless announced she would signal the start, and before Edward could get ready, she yelled "Go!" and sped away. Fortunately, Edward was able to catch up, and near the finish, they were neck-and-neck. Then, just as in the boat race, Matchless headed

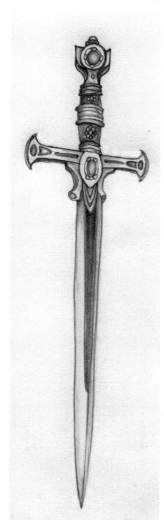

into Edward's side. He had to swerve to avoid crashing. She lunged ahead and touched the tree.

"That was truly unfair," said Edward, not disguising his anger.

"Calm down, Mercury[o], you won't be upset when you see the consolation prize. And, as our next activity, I hereby select the awarding of said prize. The elegant ceremony will take place in my charming sitting room."

Matchless led Edward to her private "sitting" room where clearly not much sitting was done. All surfaces, including chair seats, were covered with athletic equipment, including fencing epées, mitts, balls, bows, arrows, weights, riding crops, and javelins.

After digging through the rubble, Matchless found her object and presented Edward with a large, wrapped package. He opened it and beheld a razor sharp sword with a beautiful jeweled handle.

"This is fantastic!" said Edward.

[o] Mercury: the Roman messenger god, famous for his speed

"I hoped you'd like it. I was afraid if you were disappointed, you'd use it on me."

Edward laughed and took a few practice slashes through the air. "I really needed a new one. My old one got ruined cutting through the brush on the journey. Thanks."

"Don't mention it. I'm just proud that I kept the gift a secret."

"Speaking of secrets, I have one I want to share with you. The only other person who knows is Elizabeth."

"Let me guess...you're not a prince, you're a dangerous criminal disguised as a prince. I knew you were too good to be true."

"No, really. I want you to be serious. I'm an artist."

"Right," said Matchless, "and I'm a Morris dancer°."

"Please, Matchless, I want to show you my drawings."

"I think I would have preferred your being a dangerous criminal. I'd be willing to risk my life to spend time with you."

"Honest?" asked Edward.

"Well, maybe I wouldn't die for you, but I'd be willing to faint. Will that do?"

"Can't you stop joking? I'd like for us to talk."

Matchless said very quickly, "I'm not much of a talker. Just ask me a question and I clam up. Can't think of a thing to say. There aren't any words to express my thoughts. Or maybe there just aren't any thoughts."

Edward laughed and shook his head.

Matchless spoke more slowly: "Actually, I have an offer for you, and not on a used mare. You and I make a great team. Look at our successes in the fields of battle—we won the sailboat race, we won the archery tournament, we beat the pilfering° picnic ants. I hereby offer to be your teammate where it really counts. Let's sneak away to Engravia and bring the Engraver to the stone. Elizabeth will still be here plotting and planning, and you'll already have succeeded."

° Morris dancing: ancient form of folk dancing
° pilfering: stealing, robbing

"But Elizabeth and I are a team," protested Edward.

"Teammates must consider themselves equals. She thinks she's so much better than you, but look at all the mistakes she made."

"I made them, too. And she always helped me when I needed her."

"Well, you helped her, too, so you owe her nothing. She's nothing but an effete dullard° and she'll never get you across the finish line."

"It doesn't feel right to abandon her."

"Success always feels right. Winning is what counts. And don't forget how she feels about you. She thinks you're a 'competitive, greedy hog.'"

At the mention of the words, Edward felt a lump form in his throat.

"Let the people of Whitehill know who is the true winner of this race. And please, let me, not the ungrateful Elizabeth, finish at your side. I'll leave you for a few minutes to mull° over my offer." And with that, Matchless left the room.

Edward felt deeply divided, completely confused, painfully perplexed. What should he do? He had to think clearly, to make the right decision. He looked around the room, hoping to find some guidance. Then he spied just what he needed.

༼ ༽ ༼ ༽

When Prince Peerless opened the door, he found Elizabeth tossing a ball up and down.

"What are you doing wasting precious moments at this momentous juncture°?" he asked.

Elizabeth continued tossing. "I like to toss a ball. It helps me think more clearly. And I get to test my reflexes. Here, let's test...yours!" and with that, Elizabeth threw the ball at Peerless. He tried to catch it, but fumbled it.

° effete dullard: worn-out fool
° mull: think about, contemplate
° momentous juncture: critical turning point

Peerless was flustered and angry. "Let's stop this nonsense. I came to tell you it's time for us to set out."

"Don't you think you should hear my decision first?" asked Elizabeth.

"I already know what your decision is. Any reasonable, sensible person—and I consider you one—would choose me."

"Then I guess I must be drummed out of the ranks of the reasonable-and-sensible corps°. I am going to find Edward and travel to Engravia with him."

"I command you to reconsider," said Peerless.

"Perhaps, but first you must answer a few questions. How did that ball get in here? I cannot imagine you brought it."

"That's true. My sister did."

"But I thought you said you've never allowed a 'beautiful woman' in here."

"And I meant it. I do not consider my sister beautiful, so I did not lie."

"Another distinction worthy of Sir Robert. What about reading all these books? I don't think you've had enough hours in your life to do so."

"I never said I read them entirely. I read all the covers," said Peerless defensively.

"I'm beginning to see how partial truths can be very misleading. You said we 'could' be a good team together, but we just as easily 'could not.' There's no guarantee in your statement, is there?"

"I suppose not," he admitted reluctantly.

Elizabeth's eyes flashed. "I don't know if we would be a good team, but I know Edward and I *are* a good team. I'm sticking with my best bet, if he'll have me." She ran into the hall as the clock struck the hour.

કટ્ટ કટ્ટ કટ્ટ

Minutes earlier, Princess Matchless returned to her room and discovered Edward sitting in a chair he had cleared off, reading a slender volume of poetry.

° corps: unit, group

"Have you lost your mind? I'll go on a search to find it," said Matchless.

Edward looked up from his book. "Peerless must have left this. It's actually quite good and very helpful. Sometimes when things seem too complicated and difficult to understand, you need to listen to the thoughts and wisdom of others. Poetry can illuminate° great human truths. Here's a good one..."

"Please, put me on the rack, twist on the thumbscrews, boil me in oil. Just don't make me listen," said Matchless.

"I promise, it's very short and won't hurt too much." Edward read:

"Many people wander
To places far and wide,
They look for fame and fortune
And love along the ride.

They think they'll find fulfillment
Wherever they may roam,
But they o'erlook the wonders
That could be found at home."

"What is that supposed to mean?" asked Matchless.

"It means that you don't necessarily have to look afar for good things. Sometimes we undervalue the treasures around us because they're right under our noses," explained Edward.

"You have nothing right under your nose, but you could always grow a mustache."

Edward sighed, "I had a helpful, intelligent partner at my side for the entire journey, and I didn't appreciate her strengths. Maybe you and I could succeed at this mission, but I think my chances are better with Elizabeth. After all, she's a white-rumped sandpiper."

"A what?" said Matchless.

° illuminate: shed light on, clarify

"A rara avis who may seem dull at first, but who possesses hidden splendors. I just hope she'll fly away with me."

He ran out the door into the hall as the clock chimed. There was Elizabeth, hurrying out, too. The two ran to each other, embraced warmly, then parted awkwardly.

"Edward, I am so sorry."

"Not as sorry as I am," he said.

"Oh, stop being so competitive," she teased. "By the way, I'm not only sorry, I'm also wrong. I learned how dangerous partial truths can be. It's like stepping on shifting ground; you never can find sure footing. Let's tell the Engraver the whole story."

"That's great," said Edward as the clock finished chiming, "but we had better tell a quick version of the whole story. The clock just struck noon which means we have only twelve hours left!

CHAPTER ELEVEN

ENGRAVIA

As fast as they could, Edward and Elizabeth raced out of the castle, up the main street, through the gates, and down the hill to Engravia. They arrived at the iron ring at the same time and both grabbed hold to knock. They raised the ring and released it, but there was no deafening clang as expected. Instead, the door automatically and silently slid open.

"'Ladies first' is the rule," said Edward, making way.

"'Cowards last' takes precedence°," replied Elizabeth, yielding her place.

Edward stepped through the opening, closely followed by Elizabeth. As soon as they passed through, the door slammed shut.

"I guess we're truly committed," said Elizabeth shakily.

Edward pointed to a stone tablet propped up along the side of the path on which was carved:

THERE IS NO TURNING BACK ON THE ROAD OF LIFE.

They took a few steps. "I don't think I like this place," stammered Elizabeth.

Another tablet became legible; it said:

JUDGE NOT THAT YE SHALL NOT BE JUDGED.

"Shh, Elizabeth, say no more," whispered Edward.

"All right, I'll hold my tongue," replied Elizabeth.

° precedence: first place, priority

The next tablet read:

SILENCE IS GOLDEN.

In the silence they could hear a distant tapping sound. It was the only sign of life in Engravia. The massive stone wall did not surround a village, but rather an extensive sculpture garden. All over the grass were block pedestals on top of which stood life size stone figures. Elizabeth spotted the vast sculpture of an elephant and ran over to inspect it. On the pedestal was carved the inscription:

HE FORGOT.

Edward visited the adjacent° tiny mouse sculpture whose pedestal read:

HE WAS NOISY.

There were stone flowers on a pedestal stating:

THESE ROSES WERE BLUE,
THESE VIOLETS WERE RED.

And a tree sculpture read:

LITTLE STROKES DID NOT
FELL THIS OAK.

"These sculptures are wonderful!" said Edward. "Someone is a master sculptor."

Elizabeth looked pale. "I don't think anybody made these. This garden is our home for eternity if we don't get back to the valley in time."

Edward felt a pit in his stomach as he looked again at the stone figures which all had violated the terms of an engraving. He studied a cat with the inscription: SHE ONLY HAD

° adjacent: neighboring, next to

EIGHT LIVES and an old dog with the legend: HE LEARNED NEW TRICKS.

Hoping to boost Elizabeth's spirits as well as his own, Edward said, "At least there aren't any people here."

"I think you spoke too soon," said Elizabeth, who had moved ahead. She looked at a sculpture of a young girl which stated: SHE WAS PEPPER AND CHILI, AND EVERYTHING SILLY. Next to the girl, a sculpture of a jester read: HE WAS SUPPOSED TO BE A BANKER.

"He must have run off to joke and juggle, poor man," said Elizabeth.

Edward walked over to gaze at a beautiful young woman holding the hand of a shabby minstrel°. Her block read: SHE WAS SUPPOSED TO MARRY A DUKE. Beside her was a young man with his arm encircling the waist of a shepherdess, bearing the legend: HE WAS SUPPOSED TO MARRY A COUNTESS. There was also an old man with a young woman, and a young man with an old woman.

"Elizabeth, I'm afraid I've found our place in the garden if we don't alter the stone. Everyone in this area tried to defy° an engraving about marriage."

"Then let us loiter° no longer. We've got to find the Engraver and get back on the road." They ran off in the direction of the tapping, oblivious to the two empty pedestals that stood waiting in the marriage section.

At the top of a grassy hillock°, Edward and Elizabeth spied the source of the sound. On a large stone platform surrounded by thick stone columns sat a group of ten people in togas. Each person held a stone tablet and, with a chisel and mallet, chipped letters into it. The group consisted of five females and five males, varying in age from about six to sixty.

°   minstrel: traveling medieval singer
°   defy: disobey, rebel against
°   loiter: linger, tarry
°   hillock: a small hill

As Edward and Elizabeth drew nearer, they could see that all the stonecutters were seated at the feet of a tiny old woman on a stone bench. She, too, was wearing a toga and her stone gray hair was pulled back in a simple bun. She looked up as Edward and Elizabeth entered the workplace and stared at them with piercing black eyes that showed no sign of age.

"Excuse me, madam, could you tell us where we'll find the Engraver?" asked Elizabeth.

The old woman spoke in a staccato° voice, reminiscent° of the chisel's tapping. "Seek and ye shall find." She nodded at a young man at her feet who immediately put aside his tablet and took a new one from a pile. He begin carving: SEEK AND...

Elizabeth turned to Edward and whispered, "We don't have time for riddles. Where do you suppose he is hiding?"

Edward said, "I recently learned that the object you seek is often right in front of you." He whispered to Elizabeth, "I believe you are looking at the Engraver."

Elizabeth looked doubtful. She said quietly, "What a silly thought. The Engraver must be a big, strong man. Someone with the vigor to journey far and wide. Someone with the strength to carve deeply into stone." Her voice rose with emotion: "I'm sure this frail woman can barely move."

The old woman smiled and said, "Appearances can be deceiving." She nodded at a middle-aged man who began carving: APPEARANC...

Embarrassed, Elizabeth turned to the old woman and asked, "Madam, is it possible that you are the Engraver?" The old woman nodded and Elizabeth gasped.

Edward jumped in, saying, "I am Prince Edward of Whitehill and this is Princess Elizabeth of Graycliff."

"You are strangers in a strange land," the Engraver said, gesturing to a young woman who tapped out: YOU ARE STRA...

"Yes, we are," said Edward. "We have endured much to get here."

The old woman responded, "Great deeds are wrought° at great risks." A middle-aged woman began a new tablet: GREAT DE...

"We've come on an urgent matter," said Elizabeth.

° staccato: abrupt, detached tones
° reminiscent: suggestive, recalling
° wrought: carefully shaped, put together

"Ahh, time is of the essence°," said the Engraver. The oldest man in the group began carving: TIME IS OF...

Elizabeth continued, "Fifteen years ago, our advisors hired you to engrave a stone, binding us to a marriage which must take place by midnight tonight. We want you to change the stone, if it's possible."

"Even the highly improbable° is possible." A little girl began work on that one.

"Then we can hope?" said Elizabeth joyfully.

"Where there's life, there's hope." More carving.

"We've had a lot of hope, but also despair. We didn't think we could get here on time," explained Elizabeth.

"No one knows what he can do until he tries." Another tablet.

"It wasn't what each of us could do—alone we would have failed miserably—but what we could do together," said Edward.

"There's strength in union." And another tablet.

"That's what Sir Robert and Lady Claire tried to tell us," said Elizabeth.

The old woman held up her hand to pause the cutters. "I remember them well. They almost did not make it here."

"How is that possible? They're both so wise," said Elizabeth.

"Everyone has his weakness." She nodded to a young woman, who started carving. The old woman whispered, "If I recall correctly, Sir Robert's was a silver brocade tunic in Vanitonia and Lady Claire's was a dark chocolate mousse in Gluttonia."

"I cannot believe it!" said Elizabeth.

"You can always expect the unexpected," said the old woman, nodding at the young man who had finished the first carving.

"But if I expect the unexpected, then it will no longer be unexpected," argued Elizabeth.

° essence: core, intrinsic meaning
° improbable: unlikely, doubtful

The Engraver's eyes sparkled. "I love a conundrum°, don't you? My favorites are: 'The only thing I know is that I know nothing' and 'Nothing endures but change.'" She nodded at two cutters to carve the sayings. "I've spent weeks pondering those truths."

Edward interrupted. "We do not have weeks. We have but hours."

"Time and tide wait for no man." Another tablet.

"You are talking in circles. We've already established that 'Time is of the essence.' We must move forward, address the particulars," said Edward.

"But I like generalities," said the Engraver.

"We need to deal with reality," said Edward.

"But I prefer truth. My work is for mankind, not a man."

Edward persevered. "You have created a wrong and you must right it. You must travel with us to the valley to alter the stone."

The Engraver suddenly looked timid. "And what if I cannot do it?"

Edward pointed to one of the finished tablets. It read: NO ONE KNOWS WHAT HE CAN DO UNTIL HE TRIES.

"Haven't you ever changed an engraving?" inquired Elizabeth.

"On rare occasions, when a mistake was made. For example, one cutter misunderstood me and carved HASTE MAKES WAIST. Everyone who rushed around grew very fat. I had to change that one."

"You see, you can do it. We'll be there to help you. Remember…" Elizabeth pointed to THERE'S STRENGTH IN UNION. "And we're prepared to pay you handsomely, only we'll have to do it after the job is completed."

"What care I for riches?" said the Engraver with a wink at Elizabeth, and a nod to the little girl to carve.

"Do you think we can get to the stone by midnight? Do you know a secret route?" Edward asked.

° conundrum: riddle, mystery

The Engraver responded, "There are no short cuts in the Path of Life." Then she added, upon seeing two anguised, young faces, "But, luckily, there are short cuts in the path to the valley." The Engraver rose from her bench, lifted a bag filled with small tablets and tools, and took a step. She turned to her disciples, saying, "Even a journey of a thousand miles begins with the first step." The old man began carving.

Edward took her arm to gently propel° her. "And continues with the second," he said.

The three made good time through Engravia. The old woman was surprisingly spry° and quick. When they arrived at the exit, however, the solid stone door was still shut. Edward tried with all his might to push the door, but it would not budge.

"It looks like we're trapped," Edward said.

"Nonsense," replied the Engraver. She addressed the door and said in a sugary tone, "Please." It immediately sprang open. Turning back to Edward, she said in her staccato voice, "Didn't anyone ever teach you? Saying 'please' can open many doors."

❧❧❧

Outside the Engravia gates stood Prince Peerless and Princess Matchless, holding Elizabeth's travel bag and Edward's sack.

"You departed so quickly you forgot your belongings," said Peerless.

"And you forgot to bid us a tearful goodbye," teased Matchless.

"Let's forestall° the goodbyes awhile." Peerless addressed Elizabeth. "I insist that you come to judge today's dance competition. It is an important cultural event that you won't want to miss. Please come back; we are perfect individually and perfect together."

"And I hoped you would come to judge the finest tournament knights in the world. It will be a highly civilized afternoon—lots of

° propel: push
° spry: agile, nimble
° forestall: prevent, preclude

blood, lots of guts," said Matchless to Edward. "Please come, I can't live without you." She pretended to gasp for air.

"It sounds so appealing," said Elizabeth.

"Seems terribly inviting," said Edward.

"And yet..." Elizabeth nodded at the Engraver, who reached into her bag and pulled out a small tablet which read: APPEARANCES CAN BE DECEIVING. She gave it to Peerless and Matchless, whose turn it was to be speechless.

Edward and Elizabeth grabbed their bags and headed down the path with the Engraver as the Utopia clock struck one.

⁊🐚⁊🐚

Two hours later, the threesome arrived at the gates of Greedonia. King Pointless stood waiting for them by the gate. He held out a large, dirty gold sack.

In his creaky voice, he called to Edward, "This is for you and the missus."

Edward took it, discovering that the bag was heavy with gold coins. "Thanks, King Pointless, much obliged."

"That's just the beginning of my gift. Come inside and I'll give you bags of gold for all your future little ones. Think of the life they'll have. The security. The luxury." He swung open the creaky gate to admit Edward.

"It sounds awfully tempting, but I have no need for countless riches."

The Engraver reached into her bag and handed Pointless a tablet that read: MONEY CAN'T BUY HAPPINESS. When he saw it was not made of a precious metal, Pointless threw it away.

⁊🐚⁊🐚

As they neared Vanitonia, the clock chimed five. Inside the open gate, in full silver regalia°, stood Princess Flawless. She gazed in a mirror while two servants fanned her with silver ostrich feathers.

° regalia: royal ceremonial dress

In her breathy voice, she said, "As long as there's a mirror handy, one need never be bored." She addressed Elizabeth: "Here, I have a hat for you to ward off those abominable° freckles, and a fan to keep the unsightly sweat from your brow."

Elizabeth took the silver hat and delicate silver fan with a curtsy and "thank you."

Flawless continued, "What you really need, though, is a new dress. The one you are wearing is so tattered and torn. You cannot return to your people looking like a peasant. Come in and we will outfit you properly, so you can proudly face your subjects."

"It seems so alluring, but I have learned that it is more important to be beautiful on the inside than on the outside."

The Engraver held out a tablet that read: BEAUTY IS ONLY SKIN DEEP. Flawless took the plain object with a limp hand and a restrained look of disdain°.

❧❧❧

Dinnertime approached as did the smells of Gluttonia. The clock was striking seven as Queen Bottomless held out rolls and cider to Edward, Elizabeth, and the Engraver.

Edward ate quickly, ravenous° since his last meal had been breakfast.

Bottomless, who herself was eating a roll, said, "So glad to see your appetite is still hearty." Chew, swallow, new bite. "Why don't you come in? We'll serve you a proper meal. I understand tonight's foie gras with stewed figs is particularly delicious." Chew, swallow, sip of cider.

"It sounds so enticing°; I'd love to say yes. And yet, I've learned that the foolish man lives to eat, the wise man eats to live." He headed back to the path.

° abominable: repulsive, vile
° disdain: contempt, scorn
° ravenous: starving, famished
° enticing: tempting, appealing

The Engraver handed Bottomless a tablet that read: MAN DOES NOT LIVE BY BREAD ALONE. Bottomless only noticed the word "bread" and, as if it were a reminder, helped herself to another roll.

⁊🐚⁊🐚⁊🐚

By the time they reached Energia, the sun had set and the clock was chiming nine. Prince Restless was running in circles inside the gate. He stopped when he saw their approach and began stretching.

"My cup runneth over. So happy to see you. No words to express my joy. Please stretch with me. You look so weary. You need new strength."

Edward and Elizabeth shrugged, and stretched out their arms and legs. It felt good after many hours of walking.

"Swimming races are soon. Come for a dip. Think of the cool water. Think of the crowds. Please say yes," said Restless.

"I'm afraid we can't," said Edward. "We have to complete our mission in under three hours."

Restless looked disappointed. "All work and no play, makes it a dull day," he said.

Edward responded, "Perhaps. But 'Life is a balance between work and play; too much of either will drive joy away.'"

The Engraver threw Restless a tablet with Edward's words; he caught it with ease.

⁊🐚⁊🐚⁊🐚

The moon was bright, and the three advanced swiftly. As the clock struck eleven, they reached Slothonia. Three chairs with plump pillows had been placed outside the gates. Without a word, they flung themselves down. Elizabeth took off her shoes to rub her aching feet.

King Listless, sleeping on a padded bench, awoke and called in his sleepy, dull voice, "Come in. We have three fluffy down beds waiting for you with silk sheets and velvet blankets. You've earned a proper rest."

"It sounds almost irresistible," Elizabeth said, jumping up, "but we have only an hour. We cannot tarry." She pulled Edward to his feet. The Engraver left a tablet for Listless, who had resumed snoring, which read: HE WHO HESITATES IS LOST.

ॐ॰ॐ॰ॐ

A storm was brewing. Clouds collected overhead, obliterating the moonlight, and thunder rumbled in the distance. The wind began to rise. It blew, it howled, it roared. Elizabeth feared she would be pushed off the path, but the tiny Engraver led them steadfastly onward in the dark.

Finally, they slid down the hill that Edward and Elizabeth had climbed five days before. As they reached the bottom, a bolt of lightning ripped across the sky, illuminating the scene. Standing two paces away, in front of the stone, were Sir Robert and Lady Claire with an hourglass, and barely any sand was left.

CHAPTER TWELVE

The STONE

The Engraver rushed to the stone. Sir Robert and Lady Claire raised their lanterns above the carving so she could see. The stone was unchanged and read:

YOUR JOYS ARE MY DELIGHT,
YOUR WOES ARE MY SORROW,
YOUR PRESENT IS MY DAY,
YOUR FUTURE, MY TOMORROW.

IT IS PROCLAIMED AND PROMISED THAT PRINCESS ELIZABETH
OF GRAYCLIFF AND PRINCE EDWARD OF WHITEHILL SHALL
BE MARRIED FOR LIFE BEFORE THE AGE OF SIXTEEN.
THIS CONTRACT SHALL BE SEALED WITH A KISS.
FAILURE TO COMPLY WITH THE TERMS OF THIS ENGRAVING SHALL
RESULT IN THE PARTIES BEING TURNED TO STONE.

"What do you think?" said Elizabeth impatiently.

"I think...I think it is masterful work. I forgot how well I carved in my younger days," said the Engraver.

"But can it be changed?" asked Edward.

"That depends on how much time is left," she replied.

Lady Claire shifted her lantern to examine the hourglass. "Two, maybe three minutes at most."

The Engraver shook her head. "The carving is very deep. I cannot undo it in so little time."

"Then all our effort has been for naught°. Our choices remain to marry immediately or become part of your garden," said Edward.

"The garden has very nice views, and we work hard to keep the birds away," offered the old woman.

"Wait a minute," cried Elizabeth, who had been staring at the stone the whole time.

"That's all we've got," said Edward.

"Do you have time to carve one small word?" she asked the Engraver.

"Yes," said the old woman, reaching in her bag for her chisel and mallet.

"Then add the word 'not' after the word 'shall,'" said Elizabeth. "The stone will read: Princess Elizabeth and Prince Edward shall *not* be married."

Sir Robert laughed. "That's a solution worthy of me. Good show."

The Engraver stood poised to begin her work. "I think I can do it, but I must warn you, I will not tamper with the engraving again. Such enchantments are very delicate."

As soon as the Engraver began to tap, lightning flashed and the wind raged. It extinguished Sir Robert's lantern and only the dim light of Lady Claire's remained. The old woman worked with speed and accuracy. She stood back to admire her work just as the first stroke of midnight tolled.

"It is done," said Sir Robert. He turned to Edward and Elizabeth saying, "And now you must seal the new terms with a kiss."

"Oh dear," said Edward, suddenly nervous and uncomfortable. What if Elizabeth objected to kissing him? He remembered the last such encounter. "Can't we dispense with that formality?"

° naught: nothing, zero

"I'm afraid we cannot. It's still part of the contract," asserted Sir Robert, to the tone of the fifth chime.

Edward turned to Elizabeth. "Let's do it quickly and get it over with. I hope you won't mind too much."

Elizabeth was hurt by Edward's apparent reluctance. "Just proceed. I'm sure we'll both survive the kiss, but not the lack of it." The eighth bell rang.

Edward drew close, but pulled back. "This is so awkward."

Elizabeth grabbed him and pulled his head to her. At the sound of the eleventh bell, their lips met. The bell for midnight continued and finished. They kissed, and kissed, and kissed, lost in the moment. Finally Sir Robert cleared his throat and said, "I think that should be sufficient."

As Edward and Elizabeth parted, so did the clouds, and moon and star light flooded the valley. Edward and Elizabeth laughed. They danced. They hugged.

"We succeeded. We triumphed. We conquered," shouted Elizabeth.

"They said it couldn't be done, but we made the impossible, possible," hooted Edward.

"I'm free...free as a bird," said Elizabeth, twirling.

"A rara avis in flight," said Edward.

"Success hard won is sweetly savored°," said the Engraver to Sir Robert, and she began tapping out her words on a blank tablet.

"I don't know about 'sweetly,' but it's definitely savored," said Sir Robert.

"We're free to marry anybody," exulted Elizabeth.

"We're free to marry nobody," crowed Edward.

Suddenly, Elizabeth's laughter stopped. She ran over to the stone and stood before it, reading. A sob tore from her throat and her eyes filled with tears.

° savored: enjoyed, relished

"Whatever is the matter?" asked Lady Claire.

Two tears spilled over, flowing down Elizabeth's cheeks. "We endured so much to be free from the stone's obligation. But I just realized that it says that Edward and I can never marry each other." She became embarrassed by the bold implication of her words. "Not that I want us to...I just thought we had won complete freedom."

Edward's exuberance° had dissolved as quickly as Elizabeth's. He hurried over to her and took her hands in his own. "Tell me the truth. If you were free to marry me, would you?"

Elizabeth could not look into his eyes for fear he was mocking her. "What use is there in discussing it? The stone is altered and the Engraver done. You heard her say that she would not attempt any further revisions."

"I don't care what the Engraver will or won't do," said Edward. "It does not alter the fact that...your joys *are* my delight, your woes *are* my sorrow."

Elizabeth's heart swelled with happiness. "Oh, Edward, we really have learned to live not just *with*, but *for* each other. But it cannot be." She pulled her hands from his grasp. "We have destroyed all hope of a future together," she said with a few fresh tears. "You must go your way and I will go mine."

"I am surprised at you, Elizabeth. You must learn to read more carefully. How old are you now?"

"Fifteen," she sniffled.

"No, we both turned sixteen at the last stroke of midnight. And according to the stone, we shall not marry *before* the age of sixteen, but we are free to do so *after* that age."

"A fine interpretation, Sire. Simply capital!" said Sir Robert.

Elizabeth stopped crying as Edward's words sank in. "Then I can marry anyone I please?"

° exuberance: enthusiasm, excitement

"Yes," said Edward emphatically, then he added more quietly, "as long as it's me."

"That's the full extent of my choice?" she asked, smiling and drying her eyes.

"Oh no, there are lots of eligible bachelors available for you. There's King Listless of Slothonia. In your household you'll be able to say, 'There's always a dull moment.' Or you can marry Prince Restless of Energia—if he'll stand still long enough to say 'I do.' And finally, King Pointless is an excellent choice: a man who knows the cost of everything and the value of nothing. He could buy you diamonds the size of potatoes, but he won't even buy you potatoes the size of diamonds."

"You left out one other contender: Prince Peerless," said Elizabeth.

Edward grew serious. "That's because I truly fear his competition. I know he is better suited for you. I know he is perfect for you. And yet..."

"Edward, is Princess Matchless perfect for you?" Elizabeth interrupted.

"I used to dream of being with someone like her. All I wanted was a woman who was funny, athletic, and unpretentious°. But I discovered that humor without understanding, and competitiveness without integrity°, are unappealing."

"Well, I used to dream of being with someone like Peerless, but I discovered that intelligence without humor, and elegance without honesty, are unacceptable."

"Elizabeth, we may not be 'perfect' individually or together, but I think we complement° each other."

"That's a fancy way of saying we are very different."

° unpretentious: without airs
° integrity: honor, having good values
° complement: balance, together make a whole

"We are different, but that's a good thing. Together we can tackle any problem, overcome any difficulty. And we'll help each other to learn and grow."

"I suspect it will take us a lifetime to learn everything from one another."

"I'm willing to spend the time if you are. We'll broaden our horizons and discover new sources of enjoyment," said Edward.

"I would like to have as many holds upon happiness as possible," agreed Elizabeth.

"Just don't expect me to ever appreciate Gregorian chants," warned Edward.

"Fine, as long as you don't expect me to relish bloody jousts," responded Elizabeth.

"And we won't overindulge in any delight," said Edward.

"Never! We've both learned that lesson," Elizabeth said, and added, in a staccato voice, "Everything in moderation." She nodded at the Engraver, who took out a new tablet to carve.

"Well, 'everything' except love," said Sir Robert dreamily.

"And chocolate," added Lady Claire sensibly.

"Then, we are in complete agreement." Edward got down on one knee and took Elizabeth's hand. "Elizabeth, say you'll be my bride."

"Sir, you are too hasty," said Elizabeth coquettishly°. "It is customary for any young lady, let alone a princess, to ponder such decisions. Come back and ask me tomorrow."

"And will you say 'yes' then?"

"I make no promises."

"Then you leave me no alternative," said Edward sternly. He stood up. "I abhor° resorting to such measures, but to ensure your future happiness and mine, I must...command you to marry me."

"Prince Edward, how could I resist your winning ways?" she said with a laugh, and the two sealed their new agreement with a kiss.

° coquettishly: flirtatiously
° abhor: hate, detest, loathe

❦❦❦

Several hours later a celebration began, the likes of which the two kingdoms had never seen before or since. Not only were the birthdays of Princess Elizabeth and Prince Edward celebrated, but also their marriage which was both a historic *and* joyous occasion.

Edward and Elizabeth lived happily forever more, and it was said that, though their union was not engraved in stone, it was written in the stars.

here's what kids are saying about Engraved in Stone:

"*Engraved in Stone* is one of the best books I have ever read. I couldn't put it down, even to eat lunch. The way it was both funny and exciting reminded me of *The Phantom Tollbooth.*"

—Meiying T., age 11

"All the characters in this story are enchanting. Elizabeth is my favorite. She is vibrant, dynamic, and headstrong. The author presents an unusual love story against a background woven like a beautiful tapestry. I loved the story and the language of this fabulous book."

—Beatriz S., age 10

"If this book was food, it would be delicious. Readers will eat it up!"

—Jeremy F., age 9

"My mom read the book to me. I really liked it because I always wanted to know what would happen next."

—Caroline R., age 7

"The book was very interesting, fun, and great for kids."

— Johnny L., age 8

"I always looked forward to reading *Engraved in Stone*. It was well-written, engaging and funny. It is a special book that I would recommend pulling off the bookstore shelf."

—Lara A., age 12

"A fabulous fantasy that will keep your hands and eyes glued to the book."

— Jared F., age 9